The Empty Bird Cage

Short Stories

Geraldine M. North

The Empty Bird Cage
Short Stories

ISBN: 978-1-934582-78-7

Library of Congress Control Number: 2019910149

Front cover art by Riccardo.
Back cover photograph by Andraz Lazic.
Cover layout and design by Carol Phillips for
Brigid Book Works (www.brigidbooks.com).

Published by Back Channel Press
Salem, NH

Printed in the United States of America

For Bill,
Simon, and Alison

Contents

Meanwhile the world goes on.

— Mary Oliver, *Wild Geese*

The Green Jacket

Beryl Rocker finished her soft-boiled egg in its flowered egg cup, found her reading glasses under the sofa cushion, and opened the local newspaper to the Arts Section. She ran her finger down the announcements column, pausing at each line, looking for where the Friday night art openings would be held. She knew all the venues, knew the layout of the rooms and where the table of refreshments would stand. It was June and events in the summer were quite the best ones to attend. People were relaxed and the tables generous.

She wrote down the relevant details in her notebook with its cream leather cover, each entry on a new page and dated. She would attend the ArtsStudio at 6:00 p.m. to hear a gentleman read from his newly published whodunit and then move on to TreeArts for dessert at 7:00 p.m. where a local poet was reading from his third book. TreeArts was located next to Bunny's Bakery and was known for providing fresh pastries at all events. It was a fine advertising ploy for the bakery with their elegant cream puffs and buttery-layered pastries, and for the reader.

Beryl Rocker rode her Schwinn bike, still with its original streamers and wicker basket, to the ArtsStudio a little before 6:00 p.m., while people were busy setting up chairs and organizing plates of food. She nodded to several attendees she knew from other readings and stood by the table. Her mother had advised her that people in the arts were the ones to brush shoulders with. They "smell nice," her mother had said, "and they welcome anyone who might provide an audience." Neither she nor her mother had written a line of poetry or thought of recording their lives for public entertainment. Her husband, Bertie, however had left numerous pages of a book he'd wanted to publish on mycology but died before he finished the first draft. Beryl felt sad that her husband, who showed such promise in so many ways, had not achieved his dream.

At ArtsStudio Beryl moved plates here and there over the white tablecloth. "Let me help," she said. She nodded to the regulars, and as they settled in their seats she went to work. She opened her floral canvas bag under the lip of the table and quickly moved three small sausage rolls into its depths, along with a handful of freshly cut carrots and celery for the dip she had at home. She was never greedy. Her mother had told her many times to "leave something on the plate." She had always adhered to that advice but recently she felt liberated, so the last two tuna sandwiches that inadvertently tipped off the plate she popped into her bag and secured the Velcro flap.

Beryl didn't need to steal food. She considered the idea thoughtfully and not for the first time. Over the past few summers it had become an adventure, something to plan for, something to break the week's monotony. She had a nice little bank account thanks to her husband, dead these five years; his

2

skill at producing rare mushrooms in their large dark basement had paid handsomely. Whenever she thought of him, she remembered the musty earthy smell that had permeated his clothes.

She reasoned that if she was ever caught taking the food she could reasonably say, at her age, that she had early dementia and be believed. She'd never be jailed: shamed perhaps in front of her friends, but would anyone really care? This new-found gift had allowed her to learn about the local artists, the painters and writers: who was published and who was not, who was showing and who was in a dry spell. She was amazed at her own daring, her dexterity, at the sleight of hand she'd perfected, the small diversion when necessary.

Beryl felt it was polite to stay at least a half hour into any reading as a thank you. People put out good money to celebrate their event, and one needed to recognize that and at least stay to bolster the audience. She'd forgotten to bring a cushion to soften the hard metal seat, so when the novelist paused for a sip of water, Beryl slipped out the side door.

She rode her bike slowly down the road to TreeArts. The parking lot was full and she was glad she didn't drive a car. She propped her bike, gathered up her canvas bag and waited in line at the door. She found herself behind a man in a green jacket. He looked so arty, so right for an evening reading that she thought he was the poet reading that night. But, no, to her surprise, after they were admitted to the hall, he sidled up to the table of food and slid a plastic bag out of his pocket. Holding it beside the table, he scooped in four or five tiny cream puffs, his hand hiding the exact number. He didn't look down at the table but stared off into space while his right hand quickly found three pineapple slices and a bunch of grapes, which he slipped into a second plastic bag. He drew a white handkerchief out of his coat pocket and wiped

3

his hand. People around him were engaged in animated conversation and had not noticed.

He was a professional, Beryl realized, nuanced and practiced. Where had he been all these years? She came up beside him and nudged his arm. She reached past him for the plate of cream puffs and pulled it toward her.

"Don't be greedy," she whispered. She slid two cream puffs into her bag.

Green jacket didn't even glance at her. He slid his handkerchief back into his coat pocket and pulled out another plastic bag, which fluttered by his hip. Beryl realized the inner pocket of his coat had been enlarged. His coat sagged on his shoulders, and she wondered if he'd lost weight recently, though his face was ruddy and he stood erect. He looked gentlemanly, and she had a sudden image of her mother saying, "You can't be too fussy, dear. Men can be surprising." That's what her mother had said about Bertie, "Really, Beryl. Mushrooms? What a surprising fellow." And so she married Bertie, hoping he might in the end surprise her, that he might elevate her life from the ordinary to the wonderful. She found, however, that his mushrooms took up all his energy.

People had seen the poet arrive and were drifting toward him and away from the table. Beryl had handled other competitors for food before by gently nudging them away, so she moved up beside him and using her shoulder and hip pushed him gently aside. She quickly moved two more cream puffs from the large oval plate to the depths of her floral canvas bag. A last tiny meringue was close at hand and she scooped it up before closing the bag's flap. There, she thought, and that's how it's done, mister. She hoped he had seen the smoothness of her movements, but green jacket seemed not to have noticed.

"I haven't seen you before," she whispered.

Green jacket moved ahead of her. His hand, long-fingered and pale, swept up several little pastries filled with red jelly, pretty raspberry tartlets.

"Are you new in town?" she asked, her voice a little louder. Perhaps he was deaf, but there was no tell-tale amplifier behind his ear where his gray hair curled. He had a little stubble on the side of his chin where the razor had missed. Beryl swept up the last two raspberry tarts.

Green jacket paused. He looked at her canvas bag. "Leave some for others," he whispered. It sounded like a rebuke.

What impertinence. Beryl shrugged her shoulders to shed his rudeness. He was tall, and it was nice to look up into his eyes; Bertie had been at eye level and slight.

People drifted back to the table to fill their paper plates before being seated. She followed the green jacket past knots of people until they reached a quiet place by the door. "I saw you," she said, her bag hanging heavily on her arm. His coat pocket bulged. Not very subtle, she thought, though Beryl had to admire his competence. They stood on the edge of a group of women surrounding the poet, and by their enthusiastic chatter she knew they hadn't yet read his book.

She thought about the pastries and wondered if she'd made the right choice in selecting the tarts rather than staying with the puffs. She couldn't return them. Her mother had been firm in that. "They're your germs, Beryl. Don't pass them on." Her mother had witnessed Beryl's five-year-old hand returning a chocolate cupcake at her aunt's birthday luncheon. Beryl was continually surprised at how often these days her mother's voice interrupted her thoughts.

The plates of food were rapidly disappearing. "Do you come often?" His voice was little more than a whisper. His eyes raked the room then settled beyond her right shoulder to where the table stood. "I need to go back," he said.

Three bottles of white wine stood on the end of the table placed there by the poet. Beryl carried her own wine glass in her bag for just such occasions; plastic, she knew, ruined the taste. She allowed the young woman with glittering earrings to pour her a glass. "Thank you, my dear," she said, and raised her glass to the green jacket. "Will you join me?"

He looked startled and glanced at the wine bottle still held by the young woman, "Why not?" he said. The stubby plastic glass looked out of place in his hand. He was even taller than she had first thought. She looked up. His eyes were quite blue, while Bertie's eyes had been brown like his miniature portabellas.

"Cheers." Beryl sipped the wine. Nice aroma. She noted the name of the winery. The slight tension in her shoulders lessened. Why, green jacket actually smiled as he sipped from the plastic beaker.

"I wouldn't have thought," he murmured, "of having a glass of wine."

"It's a pleasant choice of white, isn't it?" They sipped their wines in comfortable silence while the audience members chose Bunny's pastries from around the table and chatted among themselves.

"Who could have imagined?" he said as he finished his wine. He tossed the plastic beaker into the wastepaper basket. "This is the first time I've shared a wine at one of these events."

"Tonight I felt like a little adventure." Beryl's socks felt hot on her feet. She wore sensible shoes and socks whenever she rode her Schwinn, and with her summer slacks she used bike clips for safety. Years before she had worn black stockings and full summer skirts. "Quite arty," Bertie would say eyeing the black stockings she pulled up her freckled legs. It was a signal that he was free that evening, that he'd attended to his mushrooms. She wondered now if it was time to return to her black stockings.

"I want something more." He patted his pocket. "Did you take all the raspberry tarts?"

"I did," she said. Should she offer to share with him? There's always a first time, her mother had said, but Beryl couldn't remember the context of her mother's words. "Try the apple slices," she suggested as she wiped out her wine glass with a paper napkin and put it back in her bag. She heard it clink against her metal bike clips.

"A good idea!" And he turned back to the table.

She liked the fall of his green jacket; the buttoned tab at his waist caused the material to flare at his hips. "Perhaps we'll meet again," she called. Her cheeks flushed at her audacity. He wore black sneakers with white laces. Bertie had felt sneakers were uncouth, and she had polished his brogues through the years and wondered at the clatter they made going up and down the basement stairs.

Beryl found she was waiting for green jacket to reply. He pulled one of his little plastic bags from his pocket and smiled at her. "Why not?" he asked. "I'm staying all summer."

His three-buttoned green jacket and black sneakers were surprisingly different. He looked like someone important, a man of talent, a writer of many books. Her mother would be proud.

"Next Friday," she called. "Mary Royal is showing her pastels at the Fritz Museum. It should be well catered, a very special Opening Event. I'll see you there."

Five in a Car

The day was hot. Heat shimmered off the road and the cicadas were deafening. The peaches were ripening fast and the work-crew had arrived early that morning to begin the heavy picking. From the kitchen window I saw Ella and her children. She stood by the front gate while her husband, Matt, strode down the driveway looking for my father. A little girl hung on her skirt and two boys stood off to the side. Ella was square and dumpy, a soft cotton hat low on her forehead and tied under her chin. The children were close in age, dressed in raggedy clothes, no shoes.

"Take them some water, Sal," mother said. I took a metal mug and a billycan of water out to them and the children separated, not a word spoken, to stand in a row. I'd heard about the Grants living in an old van near Bard Creek, but I didn't know they had three children.

"Ta," said Ella when she saw the billycan of water. "This here's James and Oliver and Shelly." She touched the head of each child as she recited their names. Oliver reached for the mug first.

His face was flushed. Ella made him pass the mug and each child took a long draft; water dripped off their chins. Ella drank from the mug last. She splashed water on her cheeks and it ran down the bodice of her dress so the fabric stuck to her skin.

"You can wait in the small shed," I said. "It's cooler there."

Ella Grant didn't look much older than me and I'd just had my seventeenth birthday.

"Ta," Ella looked around. "We'll wait here."

"At least sit in the shade then." I pointed to where the box tree threw a deep shadow. Ella moved along, shoes flapping on her heels. The three children followed in an untidy shuffle. The little girl limped badly, one leg shorter than the other, her left hip pushing out the fabric of her skirt.

I put the billycan down on the grass and steadied it with my foot.

"Ta." Ella sat cross-legged on the grass. She lifted the hem of her dress and fanned her face. Oliver put his two small hands in the billycan and brought the water to his cheeks. The other two children lay on the grass, arms by their sides, toes pointing to the clouds.

"We had a dog."

I heard his voice as I turned to leave. It was Oliver, wet hands on his cheeks, pale blue eyes staring at me.

"Did you?"

"Spotty," he said.

"Was he a good dog?" I asked.

"Nah. He got run over. Da run him over."

Ella shifted. "Don't you go telling stories, Ollie." She cuffed his head. "Always telling stories. Never know what's true or t'other."

"Is true." Shelly sat up. "Da killed 'im. Got in a fit and done it."

The sun seemed suddenly hotter on my back.

"You shut," said Ella. She didn't raise her voice. Shelly looked off beyond the orchard, toward the razorback mountain.

James rolled over onto his stomach. "I'm hungry."

"Wait 'til your Da brings some lunch." Ella's voice was sharp. She settled her sunbonnet to cut off the sun. "You can go," she said to me. "We'll wait here."

"Spotty was tied up," Oliver said.

Shelly pulled at her dress. "He couldn't do nothing. He'd broke his leg."

"Shut," Ella shouted. She was on her knees, hand raised. "You shut!"

I looked at the three children, all of them alert. I found myself tense, waiting to hear the rest of the story.

"Here's Da!" Shelly stood up and upended the billycan of water. Her father held a large brown paper bag. "Da!" Shelly called and ran toward him, an ugly lolloping gait. Neither boy moved. I expected Matt to lift the child, but he ignored her outstretched hands and she ran into his leg. He didn't look at her.

"Lunch!" he raised the paper bag bulging with fruit. They would smell the ripeness, the lush promise as he opened the bag. He handed one peach to each child. Ella settled back down on the grass, took the bag and emptied the last peaches into the folds of her skirt. The juice dribbled down the children's chins.

"No work," he said flatly. He looked at me, hard-eyed. "Your father says he's got enough hands."

"They came really early," I said and turned to go.

"Can you fetch us some more water?" His voice was deep and demanding. "Maybe a towel?" Matt spoke well. He was a Grant, one of a large extended family group that lived around Bratten. The children all went to school, finished sixth grade, proud they could read and write and take a daily newspaper. He spat the rough peach seed into his hand. "Water?" he repeated.

Ella wiped the juice from her chin and held her sticky hand away from her clothes. "A towel'd be nice," Ella said.

I gathered up the billycan. This was our farm, our fruit, our box tree they were sitting under. It wasn't my fault there was no work for him.

"Ta," Ella said, biting greedily into another large peach.

When my father first mentioned the Grant family was living in their car it seemed like the most interesting bit of news I'd ever heard. How independent it sounded. I looked back when I reached the verandah and all five of them were stretched out on the grass, eating their free lunch on our property.

A few mornings later I entered the small shed to collect a dozen eggs for breakfast. We had fifty-three Rhode Island Reds that were great layers, providing eggs for us with some over to sell to the neighbors. Oliver was crouched behind the bags of wheat like an empty raggedy-bag himself.

"What do you want?" I wasn't angry, just startled.

He edged out of his hiding place, arms wrapped round the turned-up band of his sweater.

"Did you come for eggs?" I asked.

"Yes," he said. He had a cut on his knee and his feet were dark from days of dirt. "I want some eggs," he said.

"How many do you have there," I pointed to where his small hands cradled the eggs in his sweater.

"Ma's got no money," he said. "Shelly's sick."

I grabbed a small cardboard box from the end of the bench. "Put them in here," I said.

He fumbled out three eggs. I added another three. "I like the brown ones best." He leaned on the bench and rested his fists under his chin. His face was almost as grubby as his feet. I found two brown eggs and put them on top. "One's for you," I said. "And one's for Shelly."

He looked at all the eggs carefully. "One of 'em," he said, sucking in his breath, "could've two yolks."

"An egg with two yolks is awfully lucky," I said.

"Yes'm." He settled his pants at his waist, took up the box, and trotted off up the driveway.

A week later I saw Oliver walking down Warren Road. He had a thick-bodied bull terrier tethered to a piece of stout rope. The dog almost pulled him off his feet as it sniffed a clump of grass on the side of the road, then pulled Oliver toward a wattle tree on the other. The child's arm was at full stretch. "We got 'nother dog," he called.

"What's its name?"

"Spotty," he said. "He don't have a bung leg like t'other."

The dog was all cream except for its muddy paws. Maybe it was its black nose that provided the name and then I remembered the other Spotty, the dog that got run over.

"He looks like a good dog," I said.

"Shelly died," he yanked on the length of rope. "So we got us a dog."

"Your sister died?" My breath caught in my throat. I hadn't heard about the child's death, which was unusual because news traveled fast around our small town. Little Shelly, with her misaligned leg, her lurching walk.

Oliver kicked a small stone off to the side. The dog rushed after it, nearly tugging Oliver over. "She hadda fit t'other day," he continued. "Ma said she ate her tongue."

He seemed unconcerned and I didn't know what to say. It was horrible.

The dog dropped the stone and rolled over; its spotted underbelly trembled in anticipation. Oliver knelt down and

13

scratched the pink-blotched skin. "Da took her to hospital." Oliver spread his fingers in the soft sand. "Couldn't do nothing," he added.

I remembered her running into her father's leg and falling to the ground. How he walked on without seeing her.

"Ma says we're leaving." The dog had found a stick and was working its teeth into it, saliva collecting on the side of its mouth. "Police come and all." Oliver stood on one foot, then the other.

"Where will you go?"

"Ma says we got trouble." He pulled on the lead and the dog's head snapped up. "I've got m'own egg box." He smiled for the first time. "The box you give me, for m'own things." One of his front teeth had come out and he had a sweet lop-sided smile. I wanted to reassure him that it would be alright, but when I took a step toward him the dog bared its teeth. Oliver snapped the length of rope. "Shut!" he said firmly.

The dog gave a low growl and I stepped back.

Oliver kicked the dog's back leg. "Shut," he repeated. He pulled on the leash and they ran together, boy and dog, up the dusty road.

Pass the Gravy

"Can you pass the gravy?" I didn't really like the stuff, dark and filled with unknown lumps, but it was the only way to moisten the meat. "And the cranberry sauce, thanks." The sauce came straight from the can, down the table, a red jellied mass on a chipped white plate. For a woman like me living in an old Winnebago on a friend's property a free meal was a godsend.

Saint Ambrose Church hall was buzzing. Two lines of tables running the length of the hall were filled with people in every conceivable range of dress, jeans to pressed pants, T-shirts to woolen sweaters and in the middle of each table a plastic turkey was securely anchored by small orange pumpkins. I could hear the murmurs of appreciation up and down the table blending with the chink of silverware. I poured gravy over the turkey leg and mound of gray potatoes, over the peas and carrots lumped together and passed the jug. Even though the food was cooked in bulk it was good and hot.

"You come to these dinners often?" The woman seated on my right in jeans and a worn gray cardigan spooned out the cranberry jelly.

"Some weeknights," I said. "End of the month." It was one way to pay the bills. The local hospital had done some trimming so my hours had been cut. Going from full to part time blew holes in my budget.

"I always come Fridays," the woman said. I thought she was going to lick the cranberry spoon but she handed on the sauce and I settled to my meal. Before I could have my first mouthful of turkey a commotion started at the other table. The voices were loud and someone was cursing, "Jesus, man, watchit!" It was Frankie Tuttle. I'd glimpsed him when I came in. He shouldn't have come, not in his state of mind, not after I'd seen him whipping the lamppost with his belt yesterday.

"You have a problem, Frankie," I had called then, giving him room, being careful to stay clear of his flailing arm. In primary school we'd sat side by side through Miss Western's classes, and Frankie was one of my best friends back then.

"They're coming across the wall," he'd yelled. "Get outta here, Nina!" I had stepped back. Those were his demons; I had my own to worry about.

At the Thanksgiving table, Frankie tipped back his chair so it teetered on two legs. "Righto!" he yelled. "Rightooo!" His voice was loud and jangly. His hair was a stiff mop. The whites of his eyes showed like horses' eyes do when they're spooked. Saliva gathered at the corners of his mouth.

Frankie was going to have one of his episodes and I wanted to yell "Lookout everyone!" but I stopped myself. It was like calling "fire" in a crowded theater, though I couldn't see folks running away from their hot food. Frankie must have been off his meds for days by the look of him. Why hadn't someone seen to him? Got him to the hospital? He bunked at the local Haven so someone

16

had to have known. His girlfriend, Vicky, had walked out a month or so ago and she'd told me then he was getting worse. "Never know when he's going to hit me these days," she'd said. Frankie brought his chair down heavily and folks on either side of him stopped talking. I think he knew what was happening and it was all beyond his control.

"Righto," he yelled again and flung his plate across the room. He didn't want to hit anyone, not really; he was a sweet guy most times, just crazy, gone in the head. He leapt up from his chair and it crashed to the floor. Heads swiveled. My turkey was turning cold in its gravy.

"Hey, Frankie," I called. "They after you again?" He looked in my direction. "You know you're safe here," I hoped he might recognize my voice.

"Nina?" he yelled. For a moment his eyes lost their glazed look. "Nina, that you?"

Frankie and I were close in high school but then he began to lose it, whatever "it" was. He changed, heard voices. Then he went Goth. Nasty tattoos, back and arms. He had said it took away the nagging whispers, helped him concentrate on the other things. Like the serpent emerging on the pink skin of his shoulder. "Pain does that," he had told me as I used Kleenex tissues to mop up the ooze.

I raised my hand so he could see me. "It's okay Frankie, it's Thanksgiving."

He held the front of the table, his head swinging back and forth, first watching the door and then looking for me. There was no way to change the direction of things and most people at the table understood. The course was set. The police would come soon and you hoped the good ones were working that day. You knew how it went if they weren't. Then to the hospital for a little "respite" with lots of sedation, and onto his meds again.

17

Vicky had shown me her bandaged wrist from when he'd slammed her into the wall. I didn't see the bruises on her hip but she'd described them. "I ache all over," she'd said. "He's not good for me anymore." I'd told her to leave and not give a forwarding address; Frankie had a way of tracking down girlfriends. He was lonely he'd say, and he needed company so he didn't hurt himself.

"Nina," he called. His voice echoed in the hall. The gray-haired woman seated next to him tried to pat his arm but he pulled away. "Come on, Nina, take me home." He waved to me, beckoning, pulling me in. "Come on, Nina!" There was desperation in his voice.

Bertha Marsh, in her pink frilly apron strode toward him. "You need to sit down, sir!" As head volunteer, her words had the ring of authority. "It's Thanksgiving!"

"Righto!" Frankie shouted. He was standing tall at the table, legs straddling the fallen chair, hands on his hips, defiance in every line of his body.

"You go, mate," someone shouted. "You tell them what we gotta be thankful for!" Laughter spread up the table, mainly from the men, mouths full of gravy-covered turkey. A baby started crying.

"You catch the Commies," old Ben Upstack called. He was a regular at St. Ambrose dinners and knew everyone. "Left, then right, you take them, Frankie!"

Frankie snatched up his neighbor's plate of food and held it against his chest like a shield, a butter knife clutched in his other hand. Turkey and gravy fell over his belly and down the legs of his jeans as he danced from one foot to the other.

"Cut it out, Ben, you're making things worse." It was Jay Mitchell who volunteered at the Haven on weekends, and one of the few men wearing a tie. "Give him some breathing space, will you?" He took out his cell phone. "I'm calling the cops now," he looked around the room.

"Yeah, right!" Old Ben was not having a kid like Mitchell shut him up. "You do that! They put him in a cell, a lot of good that'll do him!"

Another volunteer, red mouth tightly disapproving, tapped old Ben on his shoulder. "You eat your turkey, now Ben, or there'll be no apple pie for you later." Ben shrugged.

Bertha had reached Frankie's side. She knew not to touch him, not to stand too close. "Come on, Frankie, settle down," Bertha's voice was calm. "You're going to be okay. It's Thanksgiving, turkey time. Don't let the gravy get cold."

I could have told her he wasn't going to be okay. Frankie glared at the large plastic turkey as it swayed and bobbled on the table. Between mouthfuls, all eyes were on him. He seemed to be quieting though he still held the dinner plate against his chest.

"Don't you believe nothin' she says," a man in an orange cap shouted. I didn't recognize him from the town. "They're all fascists." Someone clapped. I could have crammed the plastic turkey down his throat I felt so angry. Couldn't he see Frankie was on the edge?

And so it happened. Frankie flung the plate like a Frisbee and hit Bertha in the face. Her eyes flew open in shock. She gave a cry and covered her face with her apron. Blood seeped into the fabric as volunteers quickly surrounded her. "Give her a chair!" someone called.

Frankie covered his ears with his hands. "Gotta get out of here," he yelled. Then he was running down the hall, shoes slapping on the old wood. "They're coming for me!"

"You go, mate," one of the men in an orange vest called to Frankie as he slammed open the side door. "You get them!"

When the door closed behind Frankie, folks took up their forks again, conversation rippled through the hall. The situation was under control. Thanksgiving dinner would be deemed a success.

"Jay," I called down to Mitchell who still had his phone in his hand. I knew Jay from his work at the Haven, his volunteering at the hospital. "I know Frankie. He'll be down at the park."

"I'll tell the dispatcher then," Jay said.

I asked for a container and packed up my meal. The woman next to me stuffed a bread roll and two foil-wrapped butters in the plastic bag. I'd finish eating later, cold gravy or not.

Frankie was down in the Municipal Park, hunched over on one of the benches, head in his hands. Where else could he go? We used to meet in the park when I was training at the hospital, and he'd share my lunch. We met when it was early spring, when the big old forsythia shrubs were bursting with color, a bank of bright yellow along the north side. I always thought of Frankie when I saw the forsythia buds open. He'd be waiting outside the front doors of the hospital. "Hey Nina," he'd call. "You need some company?" He wasn't drinking at that time and we spent the hour remembering the good days. He was at a sweet place, mouth moist and urgent, dark hair curling on his forehead, and I briefly wondered if we could be an item again, like we were in high school, before whatever happened in his brain happened.

As I walked toward the park bench I heard him talking. He was holding the shadows at bay with his hands stretched out, palms up. There was a cool wind blowing down through the oak trees, shushing like a hundred voices around him. "Back off," he was yelling. "Back off!"

"Frankie," I called. "It's me, Nina." His eyes were bloodshot, his shoulders thin inside his jacket. He was cold, shivering, frightened. "Why'd you stop taking your meds, Frankie?" I sat beside him on the bench. The metal was cold. "You've been through this before, Frankie, you know what happens now."

"Come with me, Nina, please. You can explain."

One summer after high school ended we were at the local swimming hole where the Michelin tire hung from a rope over the river. We swung out together. He wrapped his long bare legs around mine and we hit the water with a giant splash. We never got to having sex, but that day we got close.

A siren sounded in the distance. In a small town like ours the police like to put on a show. Mitchell would have told them where we were, that I'd be with him. "Frankie," I zipped my jacket up tight against my chin. "I brought you some food."

I opened the paper bag so he could smell the turkey. "It's a bit cold but it'll still taste good." I put the turkey leg into his hand and some gravy dripped down his wrist. The siren sounded louder. I squeezed the butter out of the foil and spread it on the bread roll with my finger. "Eat it now, Frankie, while you have the time." He grabbed the bread from my hand. His face relaxed, his eyes focused.

"Stay with me, Nina." He said between mouthfuls. "Do you know everyone's celebrating Thanksgiving today?"

Sweet Apple Harvest

Gwennie and Roy had arrived in town in a brown pickup truck stacked high with their belongings. They bought the apple orchard and farmhouse from old Fred Lannigan in three days, all seventy-five acres of it, sweet Macintosh and green Granny Smiths, and set up house. No children, no dog, no trimmings. Mr. and Mrs. Fergusson were the names given, though they were never married and the farm belonged to Gwennie, not to Roy as the townspeople believed.

"The tractor ready to go, gassed up?" Gwennie asked as Roy finished his breakfast eggs.

Roy brushed toast crumbs off his shirt. "Done," he replied. She knew he liked to think he was man of the house, that he was in charge. Roy was a handsome man, shorter than Gwennie, slim in the hips. Gwennie believed that clothes made the man though she was careless about herself: seams undone in places, a button gone from the front of her blouse, shoes old and comfortable.

Meanwhile Roy was as slick as a bandmaster out to please his first audience.

She loved Roy though he didn't feel the same passion. They shared a life together in two bedrooms, with Roy complaining of the arthritis that required him to sleep alone but when she came to his bedroom late, he remembered it was she who provided the roof over his head. All said, it was a good working arrangement.

While Gwennie was in town doing the weekly shop, Roy was in charge and he signed up the Pearsons when they walked into the packing shed looking for work.

"Anything going?" Tom Pearson asked.

"You done this work before?" Roy asked. He was packing apples, row by row, deftly nesting each piece of fruit in a square of paper.

"Not picking apples, we haven't," Marylyn Pearson said. "Other things."

Her husband, Tom, spoke up quickly. "We'll work hard," he said. "We need the work." They wanted out of the trailer they were living in and now Marylyn was talking about babies.

Roy knew they had no experience with ladders on hot loose soil and the heat that builds under the thick ceiling of leaves, but he signed them on. In a small town, workers were hard to come by. Gwennie knew they might also be trouble: young couple with no experience, eager to do whatever it took to make some money.

"You'll work the ladders," Roy said. "Pick the high branches." He pointed to Bonnie and Bert Houde, who were seasoned workers. "They'll show you how it's done." The other men, Jim Patterson and Bob Jenkins, waited quietly in the shade while the pudgy Brett sisters sat on their haunches in the shadow of the trees. They dropped apples into the bags they carried on their chests, straps cutting their shoulders, sweat dripping off their chins. Only the smallest thread of wind found their skin. They picked from early

24

morning until the sun hit the razorback mountain and the long whistle called them in for lunch.

Gwennie met young Tom by the shed as he and Marylyn ran water from the outside tap over their aching legs. Their first day of picking. "You'll be back tomorrow?" Gwennie threw the question over her shoulder. She took in his worn clothes, his unshaven chin. Man needs someone to look after him, she thought. She assessed his age. He was the age her boy would have been now, early twenties, fair skin.

The wiry hair on Tom's legs had picked up dust and flower spikes so the hairs shone in the sunlight: hairs thick enough to spark a fire if a match was lit near them. Roy had smooth skin, smooth legs, smooth chest. "Got to get going," she said. She had an image in her head of the man her boy might have become and sometimes the young men who came across her path brought back the pain, the memory of loss.

She drove the tractor back and forth from the orchard to the shed, bringing the bins of apples up to be graded and packed. She backed that machine up, sharp as on a one cent piece, pulling a large trailer behind, maneuvering tight angles. She wore a yellow straw hat and the men on ladders pruning topmost branches could see the hat from a distance. "She's coming!" The word would be passed and everyone straightened their backs to the chore, secateurs snipping. No one spat in Gwennie's presence.

The afternoon sun filtered heat through her straw hat. Sweat formed on her forehead, ran down her neck, gathered in the little depression at her throat. Roy had constructed an outdoor shower behind the house. He'd raised a five hundred gallon tank on four thick posts and attached a shower head. She'd hung hessian bags around on three sides for privacy and the sun did the rest. Sometimes the water was too hot, other times it was so cold goosebumps formed as the water hit her skin.

Late that afternoon when the day's work was done Gwennie pulled off her clothes as usual, stacked them neatly on the rock ledge and stood under the makeshift shower. The water was warm and refreshing. She was soaping her body when Tom appeared around the edge of the hessian-bag wall. She paused, Lifebouy soap in hand, and turned her back modestly. Over her shoulder she watched the flush rise in young Tom's face.

"You want something?" she asked. "You lost or something?"

"Heard the spill of water," he said. "Thought a tap was running." He stared and Gwennie remained still, aware of her breathing, the spit of water on her shoulder.

"Where you at?" It was Marylyn's voice, sharp edged like her hips.

Tom vanished from Gwennie's sight. She ran the soap slowly over her hips, her thighs. She rubbed the soap between her hands until a lather formed, then she washed her face of sweat and dust. Young Tom's startled face remained in her thoughts. There it was again, those thoughts that confused her, the picture of her boy grown and the young man who stood beyond the shower, always a reminder of her loss.

She needed to be out of the heat, needed a cool beer on the verandah and some conversation with Roy about practical things. She needed to shake those images loose from her mind. The baby had been an unwelcome surprise, the result of the smooth-tongued high school teacher who wrote her sonnets and ran his hand under her skirt. There were no photos of her little boy, but in the top drawer of her dresser she kept the newspaper article about his drowning. They said it was neglect, a terrible accident. Sometimes she remembered the small body in her lap, felt a small hand playing with her hair.

Gwennie wrapped a large towel around her body, picked up her clothes and walked up to the house. All the workers were gone.

The shed was silent, dust motes hung in the cool afternoon air. She heard Roy clattering plates in the kitchen. Past the front gate where the jacaranda tree leaned, she saw Marylyn and Tom walking up the road to their truck.

The next day newly spun cobwebs still held dew when Gwennie stood on the back verandah. She wondered how the magic happened. Every summer morning the sun flared up and over the razorback mountain to flood the farm with golden warmth.

The Pearsons arrived. Tom waved a good morning as he and Marylyn headed for the big shed. The hairs on Tom's legs picked up the drops of dew as he passed through the grass.

"Top field," she called.

The Brett sisters gave them shy smiles as Tom and Marylyn joined the group. Gwennie reached for her straw hat and pulled it low on her forehead.

"Go gentle," Gwennie said. "Apples bruise easily."

She stepped up on the tractor and started the engine while the pickers sat around the edge of the trailer, legs dangling, glad of a ride down to the block of tall, leafy Macintosh trees. Roy, who usually worked in the packing shed, chose to work with the picking crew that day. "I need a change," he said. "Packing shed gets hot mid-afternoon."

Gwennie worked the top orchard straight through lunch. The afternoon heat was at its highest when she thought of taking a break, a long draft of water in the packing shed.

The Radford brothers, big, strong men were boxing the apples on either side of the grading machine when they heard the cries. They paused at their work. "You hear that?" they chorused. Gwennie ran to the tractor.

"Accident!" Bonnie Houde was on the path and waving her straw hat. "Accident!" she yelled, pointing down the far row of trees. The pickers had gathered in a mob around Tom, who lay on the hot ground, two ladders lying off to his side.

Roy was kneeling beside Tom. He called up to Gwennie over the noise of the tractor's engine. "He's out to it."

"Tom was picking high, ladder seemed okay." Bert Houde, the oldest picker said. "We heard a branch break, a yell. Next thing we saw he was on the ground, ladder on top of him." The story came in pieces, each worker adding and embellishing as each one's view of the accident sharpened.

Gwennie saw Marylyn's white face beyond Roy's shoulder. She brought the trailer alongside Tom's body. "Load him up," she called.

The men struggled to lift him high enough to settle on the trailer. "Go carefully," she said. Tom's face was gray. There was a gash along the side of his head, a drool of spit at the side of his mouth. He looked so young, so vulnerable. She wanted to gather him up and hold his head against her chest but she didn't move. The image came to her suddenly of the small wet bundle in her arms, the towel she'd wrapped around him, the water gurgling as the bath drained. She held her hands steady on the wheel, foot on the clutch.

"Put him on his side," Bert Houde advised. This was serious, not some splinter in the palm of a hand, a broken arm. It was twenty miles to the local doctor, thirty miles further to the country hospital.

"I'll need someone to come with me," Gwennie said. "Keep him from choking."

Bonnie Houde, tall and strong, pushed her shirt sleeves up her arms. "I'll come." She climbed on the trailer. Once trained as a nursing assistant, Bonnie could wrap a sprained ankle in seconds or tie up a wrenched shoulder with a man's belt. Gwennie knew she was the best choice. "Need to get going," Gwennie said.

"Wait up, I'm coming," Marylyn called. She climbed onto the trailer and pushed Bonnie aside. "He's my husband, right?"

Everyone moved back. "Right." Bonnie stood down with the other pickers. "Better call the doctor from the house, Gwennie. First thing."

"Fruit has to be finished," Roy shouted. "Nothing more we can do now. Everyone back to work."

Gwennie drove up from the orchard, low gear, fully aware of the unevenness of the track to the house. This accident would slow things down. If the storm came in as predicted they could lose the fruit and hundreds of dollars. She looked back at Marylyn crouched over her husband, swaying with the push and pull of the trailer.

The Radford brothers came out from the shed. "What can we do?" they called.

"The house. Get him inside."

The men lifted Tom off the trailer. They carried him up the house steps and through the side door.

"Where do you want him?" they asked.

Her bedroom was closest. Gwennie pulled back the quilt and they rolled him on his side. She put a pillow behind his back. Color was coming into his face. His breathing was stronger. Blood had dried in the roots of his hair in dark red flakes.

The brothers started to leave the room. "A nasty accident," one of them murmured as Marylyn waited at the bedroom door. "Sorry, sorry."

"Carrier comes at five," Gwennie called. "Have the boxes ready for loading." The men hurried down the steps, glad to leave her in charge.

Tom lay in a fetal position. Gwennie stroked his hair and ran her hand down his cheek. He was breathing. Not like the other time. And he was dry. She ran her hand down his shoulder. He was dry.

"Keep your hands off him," Marylyn's voice was shrill. "Stay away from him! Old cow!"

Her words shook Gwennie. She saw herself in the long mirror by the bathroom door. Her hair was disheveled; face red from exertion, a button undone on her shirt so the gray of her bra showed. She looked old, older than she believed herself to be. Not like anyone's wife or mother, just a worn-down, working woman with a farm to run.

"I've seen you watching him." Marylyn said. She pulled the quilt up to cover Tom's shoulder. She sat on the edge of the bed and held her face in her hands. "What am I going to do?" she muttered.

Gwennie felt drained, stained by memories. "I'm phoning the doctor."

"He's not going to die, is he?" A small girl's voice.

"It's only a head wound." Gwennie turned at the door. "You take good care of him, Marylyn, you hear me."

Three Daughters

Helen Matthews turned her needlework hoop and considered her three daughters in the cool afternoon light. She had summoned them because she was anxious about where to place their father's ashes. They sat across from her on the sectioned sofa: Natalie, the eldest, had ironed the crease in the sleeves of her blouse to a knife-edge; Sarah, the middle daughter, had shucked off her sandals to display her bright blue toenails; and Mimi, her youngest, displayed a newly tattooed string of hearts on her right leg.

Really, Helen thought, and not for the first time, *Where did my daughters come from?* She drew the wool through the coral flower on the pillow cover. Her needlepoint was advancing nicely, multi-colored peonies embedded in a circle of leaves.

Once her daughters were teenagers, they'd moved away from her. It had happened when James was ill, when all her energy was spent on his needs. The disease had progressed so rapidly, so silently, that the months flew by and before she knew it she was writing his obituary and packing his shirts in boxes for the thrift store. James had died and now her daughters had come to help bury his ashes.

Helen felt the weight of this decision. It was a long time since she'd seen the girls.

"Honestly, mother," Natalie said. "Where *should* we put daddy's ashes?" Helen had hoped Natalie, being the oldest child, would be the decisive voice in this situation. All three daughters lolled on the sofa, waiting for her answer.

Helen shrugged. "I can't decide. And that's why you're here." She moved her feet on the hassock. Her joints were stiff from sitting.

James had loved the little creek that ran down behind the house. He had taken the girls there when they were young and gathered polliwogs and frogs and dug up maidenhair fern for transplanting into the damp garden by the tool shed. James had also cherished the line of pink Rugosa roses he'd planted along the back fence, zealously watering and fertilizing them until they formed a thick hedge that became covered with flowers in the summer. And it was James who built the elaborate brick barbeque for his summer cookouts, holding court while he flipped hamburgers in one of her floral aprons.

Helen rather enjoyed having the elaborately carved rosewood box nearby and the thought that James was still close to her made her smile. She had moved the rosewood box around, first on the kitchen windowsill, then to the dining room window overlooking the locust tree he had planted, then to the living room above the gas fire. The polished wood of the container looked well in all those places and she'd decided that when it was emptied, she would keep the box. James wouldn't care if she kept paper clips and safety pins in it, and she could hear his hearty laugh, "Really, Helen, how sensible of you to use it that way."

She passed the needle several times through the canvas. Another petal finished.

"You have to decide mother." Natalie smoothed her short, black skirt. "I only have this weekend free from the library. I *am* Circulation, you know." Natalie had married and divorced within four years without consulting them in any way. She had always had her head buried in a book, and here she was, at twenty-eight, head of something in a small suburban library.

"I know, dear, I know how busy you are." Helen pulled a strand of coral wool from her sewing basket. She squinted as she threaded the needle.

Natalie stood abruptly, and Sarah sprawled into her space on the sofa, bare feet angled on Mimi's lap. "Ugh," Mimi pinched her sister's toe. "Your toenails should be pink to match your finger nails." She began to tweak each toe, "*eenie, meenie, minie, mo,*" she sang. Mimi, who was three years out of high school and tired of studying real estate, had announced she wanted to attend college somewhere far away and exciting.

"Cut it out," Sarah pulled her feet away. "Let's get dad's final resting place settled. Mother?" Sarah, a dedicated nurse, was worn out by her need to heal everyone, to give a home to every stray cat she found. She had begged Helen to take one of them, a little striped creature that became her beloved companion. Miss Tabby, Helen remembered, would soon need to be let out for her evening prowl.

"I'm thinking," Helen said. "Don't rush me." She stabbed the needle through the peony's dark center.

"Okay, mother," Mimi ran her fingers through her hair until its spiky ends stood up like a cockatoo's crest. "Do we need a shovel?" She was relieved Mimi hadn't yet put a ring in her nose or a tattoo on her forehead, but why did Mimi have to have a new tattoo every time she came home to visit? What part of her hidden life was she trying to tell them?

"Can we get on with it?" Sarah was more like James. She had his light straight hair, which on him had fallen on his forehead and on his middle daughter hung down her back in a thin braid. Sometimes Sarah wound it round her head and looked like a Fraulein.

Helen rolled the canvas around the wool and held it on her lap. She heard the small needlepoint scissors slide off her lap and drop on the carpet.

If they buried James' ashes beside the barbeque or in the rose beds, they would need a shovel, Helen realized. "The tool shed," she said. "There's a shovel there."

"I'll get the shovel," Mimi said. Why, she wondered, were the girls not more solicitous? They hadn't asked how she was feeling, whether this was a difficult decision for her. Had they ever really cared about her, about her situation? Whether she missed them?

They were foreign to her. *I don't know them at all*, Helen thought, as Natalie and Sarah stood and linked arms and Mimi slammed the door behind them. They hadn't become the adults she'd expected. All those early indications of brilliance, of stability, of promise, had come to naught. They were not necessarily disappointing, they were just less than she had originally believed possible for them. "Heavens knows, their genes are good," James had said after one of her outbursts, "Give them time, Helen, they might surprise you." Was it the age-old conundrum of mothers and daughters that made them act so lovingly to their father, so carelessly with her?

"One thing we know for sure," Natalie said. "He never wanted to be buried in a graveyard." When had that conversation taken place? Helen couldn't remember a similar conversation with James. She felt hurried and anxious. Why hadn't James confided in her? Of course, they had never expected to die, so they'd never discussed what one should do about it.

"Mrs. Mathews, time for supper. Mrs. Mathews!" And why would her daughters be so formal. They always called her mommy, or mumsie. Intimate names she recognized.

Helen's needlework lay neatly rolled in her lap. Her eyesight was a little off-focus. Had she fallen asleep? She looked around for her daughters and found a large, round woman standing before her chair. She recognized the brightly colored smock and white sneakers.

Helen struggled to rise. The girls, she wondered, where had the girls gone? The carved rosewood box sat on the round table by her side. She touched the lid. Of course they would spread James' ashes down at the creek. She would tell Mimi to put the shovel back in the tool shed and the girls could take her there this afternoon. She felt very peaceful. The decision had been made.

"Mrs. Mathews! I've brought your supper." The white sneakers shifted. Helen smelled roast chicken and heard the metal tray clang as it was placed on the table by the window.

The brightly colored smock moved to her side. "My, now, look at how much stitching you've done today." The sneakers took a step forward. "We'll put Miss Tabby's ashes back on the mantelpiece, shall we?" The rosewood box was taken away. "We all know how you like to have your dear Miss Tabby close by."

"Ah! Miss Tabby." She had forgotten. "Thank you, dear, that's a perfect solution." She allowed herself to be helped to her feet. "Perhaps tonight my daughters can join me for supper, too," she said.

Ferreting

We were coming home from school, Will and Topper and me, down along McLaren Street to where the only crossing light in town blinked. Will pressed the button and we waited impatiently for the light to turn green.

"Now!" Topper yelled, and we slid our feet over the edge of the curb.

"Nah." Will sent a silver gob of spit into the road. Today it landed just where he aimed, on a distant crack. Last week Will turned twelve and he blew out the candles on his cake in one long breath. He was my oldest brother. Topper got his name because when he was little he wore the top hat our father had used in theater, back when he was young, back before mum died.

The lights changed. We shot across the road, jostling to see who landed first on the opposite curb. The first one to reach the curb had power for the day, had the right to lead down Drury

Lane, the right to call the shots. I was always overtaken by my older brothers. My legs were shorter, my jump not as long.

Will hit the curb first, so he pulled ahead and we had to follow duck-like behind him. I noticed our shadows, long and thin, overlapping and bigger than we could ever be. Will's schoolbag looked like a suitcase, huge and bulky, and it pulled his shadow to the side, made it overlap Topper's so their shadows were joined. And my brothers were joined. Born twelve months apart, they were almost twins. They were also rivals, always fighting over something: who had the larger sandwich, the biggest blister, the worst pain in the gut. And Topper always seemed to fight harder than Will.

My shadow barely touched theirs. I was their younger sister, Birdie, and I was nine.

We walked single file down Drury Lane and past the brick wall in front of the town library. I saw a small figure in a brown sweater perched on the wall, his arm raised, just as a stone landed on Will's shoulder. Will let out a yelp and jumped to the side.

The small boy clapped his hands. "Good one!" the boy yelled. "And that's for you all!" He stretched his mouth wide with his fingers and stuck out his tongue. He looked like a fat brown toad.

He threw another stone at Topper that clipped his leg. "Got you, too!" the little toad yelled.

"Go round the back," Will whispered. Topper ran off while Will and I stayed to taunt the unknown boy.

"I'll come up and get you," Will shouted and ran at the wall, pretending to climb the bricks. "You just wait."

The small boy grinned and threw another stone. I ducked but it clipped my ear.

"Sloth," he called down. "Name's Sloth Anderson."

He had a lisp. "What?" I yelled.

"I'm Sloth," he repeated.

What sort of name was that? We knew everyone in town, but during the summer holidays folks arrived and we only got to know them after school started.

"I'm Birdie," I called back.

He looked at me with round brown eyes. Then he disappeared. Topper had pulled him off the wall. We heard Topper shouting, "Let go, you little pustule, let go." Our father was the local doctor, so we knew medical words and kids at school stood in awe of our vocabulary.

Topper brought him out the library gate and my brothers held his arms while I inspected him. He was probably my age but chunky.

"I'm new in town," he said. "Mum *shaid* to be friendly." His lisp was more pronounced. "Got your attention, tho'," Sloth grinned. I liked the way he wasn't cowed by my brothers.

"Well," Will's voice was stern, like father when he lectured us. "You don't throw stones for one thing. That doesn't make friends." Father had no time for foolish actions. My brothers eyed Sloth. I knew they were figuring out how to punish him for his stone throwing.

"You'll have to prove yourself a friend," Topper said. He liked rules and more especially liked making others follow those rules.

Will nodded, "Right." I wondered what my brothers were planning.

"Pelson's?" Topper looked at Will and I saw they were in agreement.

Mr. Pelson owned a farm a half mile down the road from us. It was where we went for eggs and fresh vegetables. Sometimes he gave us skinned rabbits for supper instead of payment for our father's medical service. Mr. Pelson had ferrets that he used to flush out rabbits. "Put the ferret down the burrow and the rabbits come charging out and into the waiting net," I'd heard him explain. My brothers had talked about borrowing one of Mr. Pelson's ferrets to trap the rabbits in the field behind our house. We had plenty of burrows to send a ferret down and free rabbits, too.

"You know where we live?" Topper asked. "The surgery on Madson Avenue?"

"Sure," Sloth nodded. "My mum's been there already." I hoped his mum wasn't really sick, but there was no time to ask.

"Sunday morning," Topper said. "Pelsons are Presbyterians, they'll be at church."

We didn't go to church. Our father was not a church-going man, so Sunday was one long day of outside play, bike riding, cricket games, whatever we chose to do as long as we did it quietly and outside the house.

It was hot in Pelson's shed and the cages were quiet, the ferrets asleep. We crouched behind a stack of wooden boxes, listening to the silence. Large bits of machinery leaned against the back wall and bags of wheat and cartons of animal food were stacked by the rabbit cages near the door. The shed smelled of dust and animals.

"Should we do it?" Topper asked. His white face glowed in the light coming through the back windows. Topper was afraid of stray animals, of catching colds, of failing math. I often thought that being a middle child wasn't such a good place to be. First and last were best I'd decided long ago.

Sloth has to do it," Will said. "He threw the stones."

Mr. Pelson had three large cages with a ferret in each one. I'd watched as they ran around their cages, seeming to copy each other's moves, their bodies sleek and feral and fascinating.

"Keep away from them, Birdie," Mr. Pelson told me when I came around to his farm one day for freshly pulled carrots.

"They'll take off a finger soon as look at it." That night I'd looked up ferrets in the encyclopedia and I found they were like polecats or prairie weasels. *To ferret out* meant to search out enemies and unfriendly ones, and as we waited I wondered if my brothers thought of Sloth as an *unfriendly one.*

"It'll get me." Sloth didn't sound as brave as he'd sounded up on the wall.

"Nah! It's asleep. You'll take it by surprise," Will whispered. "It's in that little hammock-thing. Grab it all. Two hands!"

Sloth took a deep breath. I imagined he was counting to five or ten, calming himself. He took our father's old shirt in his two hands and crept closer to the nearest cage. I couldn't see the beast but I could smell the musty odor of its sleeping place and the rotten stems of carrots and celery, the beast's droppings.

"Grab it by the back of its neck," Topper said. "But do it quick." He sounded nervous.

"Okay." Sloth's voice was muffled. "Who's going to open the door? I can't do that, same time grab the thing."

"You do it, Will," Topper said. "Open the door for him!"

Topper sounded like our father ordering me to take two Tylenol after I sprained my ankle. I was surprised because I expected Will to assert himself as leader. "Do it, Will," Topper repeated. I guessed Topper was afraid of the ferrets. I knew he didn't like to touch frogs or dead birds, and when a bat got caught on the patio curtain last year he screamed.

Will unlatched the cage door. The hammock shifted. Sloth pounced. He gathered up the hammock and the wriggling ferret in one movement, cloaking the beast in our father's old shirt. He swung it downward and shook it, then tied a knot in the top. He was economical in his movements. The thin cloth of the shirt jumped and wiggled in his hand. Sloth had proved himself as he held the bundle aloft.

I was filled with admiration for Sloth until he howled and dropped the bundle.

The knot unraveled and the ferret lunged between Topper's feet. Topper jumped. Sloth held out his hand showing pinpricks of blood on his palm.

"The ferret," Will cried. "Behind you, Birdie! Get it."

What did he expect me to do? Where had it gone? It could be anywhere. "I can't see where it went," I yelled.

"Look what you've done, Sloth," Topper yelled. He grabbed Sloth by the arm and shook him, but Sloth kicked out and struggled free. I'd seen Topper like this after I broke his Star Wars laser sword, and I didn't like him when he got angry.

"No good getting upset, Topper," Will said. "We've got to think this through." This was one of our father's favorite sayings. *Getting angry solves nothing*, father would say.

Sloth sat on a box and cradled his hand against his chest. "It hurts." He was almost in tears. I took father's shirt and wrapped it around his hand, using the sleeves to tie it in place.

"I'm sorry," I said. "It wasn't meant to go wrong like this."

"I'm not very lucky," Sloth wiped his nose on his sleeve. "I'm slow about some things."

The cage door hung open, the little hook that latched the door dangled. "It could have escaped on its own." Will's voice was firm. "We'll have to take an oath of silence, okay."

"It was his fault," Topper said angrily. "He started it. He threw the stones."

"Hands out in front," Will ordered. We formed a small circle around Sloth and reached our right hands into the center, Will's hand first, topped by Sloth's left hand, then Topper, then me last. I was filled with dread. We all knew our father believed in swift punishment after a lecture that could go on for ages. We usually received a weekend's grounding, which was unbearable

42

in the summer, less so in the winter. But it was the lecture that really hurt.

Sloth's cheeks were wet.

"He'll have to have a tetanus shot," Will said. "How do we tell dad?"

I remembered the rabbit cages. "The rabbits," I said. "He could have been patting the rabbits. You know how cranky they get."

"Brilliant." Will rarely gave me a compliment. "That's the story. A rabbit bit him."

In that moment of quiet reflection we heard scratching and scraping from among the boxes. "Run," Topper kicked over the box Sloth had sat on. "Fast!" We ran out of the shed and across the field. My heart was thumping. I was sure the Pelsons would return from church early and catch us.

Just short of our front fence we stopped to catch our breaths.

"It's no good," Will was bent over his knees catching his breath. "Ferrets are expensive. We'll have to own up to dad. Take our punishment." Will had a conscience and a mind to things that made money.

"Birdie was the reason we did it." Topper jabbed my sternum. "You were the one told us about the ferrets."

Topper blamed me for everything that went wrong. Ever since our mother died he blamed me. I was only three then, so I didn't know her like my brothers did. I had her embroidered pillow and a stiff little bear and father always said I was as pretty as my mother and bright as a button like her, but sometimes it wasn't enough.

"You're rotten, Topper," I said. "You're just chicken!" I waited for Will to agree with me, to stand up to the truth. *Truth to power* was one of his favorite sayings.

"Dad'll go easy on Birdie, he always does," Topper continued. He turned and looked at me. "You're the youngest and you're spoiled rotten."

"Leave Birdie alone," said Will. "We've got to think this through."

"I still think Birdie should own up." Topper pulled up a handful of weeds.

"My fault." Sloth was standing at my side. "I threw the stones." His lisp was more pronounced now and *threw* became *frew*. He was breathing through his nose in little wheezes and he looked pale and small beside my brothers.

"We were all in it," Will said finally. "Come on back to the house. I'll talk to dad."

"The rabbit story is best. The ferret'll come back when it's hungry." Topper stood with his hands on his hips, blocking Will's path. "I don't want another grounding when it wasn't my fault." Standing together, I saw that Topper was as tall as Will and bigger in the shoulders.

"What if it doesn't come back?" Somehow I was holding Sloth's hand.

"Okay, okay," said Will. "But we have to stick together on this rabbit story, okay?"

We formed a line and straggled across the last of the field and in through the gate to our front porch.

"You two wait here." Will was in charge again. "Come on, Topper."

Father was in his study. Through the open window we heard Will explaining what had happened, with Topper supporting the lie. "We shouldn't have gone to Pelson's farm when we knew they were at church but our new friend Sloth had really wanted to see the rabbits. Birdie told him about them. We thought that would be harmless, but one of the rabbits was crotchety and Sloth caught a bite." Will was convincing. He worked on the school newspaper and had a naturally creative mind.

"Come on in, lad, let's take a look," Father called out the window. I went with Sloth while my brothers settled in the

44

wicker chairs on the porch. He stumbled a little across the doorstep into the surgery so father helped him up on the examining table and peeled away the shirting. "Nasty," my father said. He was not in his usual suit and tie but in his weekend clothes. He was more my father and less the town Doctor. "You're very brave," he said as Sloth looked at the tooth marks on his hand. The blood had dried but the skin looked swollen. "Just a prick and you'll be fine." My father prepared the syringe and Sloth and I looked steadily out the window.

"My fault." Sloth spoke up. "I threw the stones and let the ferret escape."

My father withdrew the needle and paused. "Not a rabbit?" He turned to the sink and washed out the syringe. "So tell me what really happened, Birdie."

There was nothing else to do but tell him the real story. How Sloth had thrown stones at us and the brothers had to punish this bad behavior. How we only wanted to borrow the ferret so we could catch a rabbit like Mr. Pelson did. That we had planned to give the ferret back. I realized I was very tired and I didn't want Sloth to get in trouble. I turned and put an arm around Sloth's shoulders. "He was only trying to make friends," I said to my father.

When it was done, the bandage bulged like a giant carbuncle on the end of Sloth's narrow wrist. Father finished his mini lecture with a "Don't do anything like that again." And Sloth and I joined the brothers outside.

"Will," I said, "Dad wants to talk to you." I included Topper in a sideways glance.

They'd obviously overheard some of the conversation, because they both jumped to their feet and hurried into the surgery.

"Come on," I said to Sloth. "You need to get home and rest." I almost suggested taking Tylenol for the pain but remembered my father had done that already.

We stepped off the porch together, and as we walked through the front gate Sloth turned to me. "Mum said I'd find a friend after school started." I couldn't detect a lisp when he spoke. "I really like your name, Birdie."

In Company of Chairs

Mary Hudson clearly heard the tap-tap of her walking stick and the late afternoon chattering of the crows. She entered Wallington Park where the oak trees cast long shadows that sliced up the lawn. She stopped by the bandstand that was built after the town fire amid much debate over cost and whether the roof should be flat or peaked. The nearby swings swayed though the children had long vanished. Mary hunched her shoulders against the crisp breeze.

A dozen plastic lawn chairs sat on the grass in front of the bandstand. It was unsettling, that circle of white chairs. They were whispering, like they had secrets to tell. She was sure she heard children's voices again, and the chairs seemed to shuffle across the grass and nudge each other. She remembered the plastic chairs stacked against the wall of the abandoned building, how she and the other children had taken them down to play. They must have been seven or eight then. There was an argument taking place, some pushing and shoving.

Mary was not a drinking woman, not on a Sunday afternoon after early Mass. She was on her way home to watch her favorite TV show, but there were the chairs, set out in the park, seemingly forgotten. She'd had a late lunch and this evening two hard boiled eggs waited for a little salt and a slice of her homemade wheat bread. Why, Mary wondered, had the chairs not been stacked and carried off? Will Fortnum was paid to do that. She knew his number at the Town Hall, but on a Sunday no one would be there. She had half a mind to go calling; she knew where Will lived, since they'd known each other their whole lives.

A golden retriever, tail held high and fanned out by the breeze, came through the gate and sniffed around the legs of the chairs. "Come here boy." It was Will Fortnum pushing the metal gate closed, calling his dog. His dark overcoat blended into the shadows. He held a leash in one hand and a pipe in the other.

"Why, Mr. Fortnum, I was just thinking of you." Mary took a step forward and leaned on her walking stick.

"Are you taking your constitutional, Miss Hudson?"

"After meetings, shouldn't these chairs be stacked up and stored?" Mary watched as two chairs seemed to move closer together. "How come the chairs are still here, Mr. Fortnum?" The dog paused at the sound of her voice and lifted its head.

The old man looked surprised. "Why, how could this happen?" He walked over to a white chair with broad arms and sat down. "Come, Bruno." He slipped a treat from his pocket into Bruno's waiting mouth. "Isn't this the best time of day, Miss Hudson?"

Mary leaned over and patted Bruno's sleek head. "The chairs, Mr. Fortnum?"

"Someone forgot the rules." Will snapped the leash onto the dog's collar. "Take the weight off your feet, Miss Hudson, sit for a minute."

Mary settled into a plastic chair and stretched out her legs. The grass had not been mown recently and it made a soft little bed for her heels. The other chairs remained in a circle. The streetlights had come on and were throwing short shadows on the grass.

"I just finished my afternoon walk." Mary tightened her scarf and settled her coat over her legs. "It's getting chilly." She thought of her warm little apartment, the boiled eggs waiting, her favorite program ready to start. "I thought," she began. "I thought I heard the chairs talking." She laughed apologetically. "Funny, the way one's mind works."

"It's that time of year." Will took out his pipe and banged it against his leg. Remnants of tobacco fell to the ground. "Those crows surely make a racket, don't they, Miss Hudson?"

"I remember," Mary began, "when we played here as children. Do you remember, Mr. Fortnum, before the bandstand was built, before it was even thought of? Who needed a bandstand when the band stood out on the grass and we all sat on blankets, picnic style."

"Those were pleasant times, Miss Hudson."

The wind gathered up an abandoned paper bag and it caught against one of the chair legs. Mary thought she saw the chair move, daintily freeing itself. She wiped her eyes. "All we talked about then was the new bandstand. Until we had the fire."

"It was so, Miss Hudson. The bandstand was built before the fire, along with the new library."

"I do like the new library, though the lights could be stronger." Mary said. "Wouldn't you think the trustees could put better lights in the reading room?"

49

"You'd think so, Miss Hudson, you'd really think so."

"And then we had that terrible fire, Mr. Fortnum. Who could forget how that vacant building burned. And then Diamonds Department Store caught fire."

"We were children then, Miss Hudson. Our teacher brought us out to Nelson Street and we lined the footpath and watched the flames." He held a match to his pipe and for a moment the smoke smelled comforting. "Matches, our teacher said, could have started it all."

Bruno got up, stretched, and settled again.

"Diamonds was the only place in town that sold hair ribbons and buttons. It was sorely missed." Mary replied. "We had to drive all the way to Newport after that." She paused. "A trial for us all, with the price of gas back then."

Mary put her hands in the pockets of her coat. The chill was settling into her bones. She'd have to get going, put on the kettle for a hot cup of tea. The chairs were moving again. One of them turned around in a circle and settled again. Remarkable, she thought, they must be feeling the chill, too. "I can't forget," Mary said. "The fireworks went off inside that empty building like the Fourth of July had arrived early."

"Such a terrible accident." Will cleared his throat.

"He went missing after the fire, Mr. Fortnum. It was sad for everyone."

"A very sad time, Miss Hudson, indeed it was."

"Remember how they searched the river? Boats and lights on all night. Divers coming and going. They never found his body, did they, Mr. Fortnum?"

"No, Miss Hudson, they didn't. And it wasn't for lack of searching."

"What do you think happened, Mr. Fortnum?" Why didn't she stop talking? It was so long ago. They'd been children back then.

It had been a fearful year. Parents called their children in off the street before dark; ball games were left unfinished; hopscotch taws were left on the pavement.

Bruno rose and sniffed the air. "Looks like Bruno's ready for his supper." The halo of smoke from Mr. Fortnum's pipe hid his face for a moment. "I'd forget the fire, Miss Hudson. Nothing could be done. It happened and we all have bad memories."

Mary's thoughts returned to the vacant building. The windows were boarded up. Jenny, Colin, Will. Then Billy Costa joined them and Peter came in late. Colin, the new boy, had older brothers. That's where he got the cigarettes. "Stay a little longer, Mr. Fortnum, just until I rest a bit." Around her the chairs appeared to be agitated.

Will stretched his shoulders and crossed his legs. Bruno settled again at his feet.

"Colin Marshall." Mary folded her arms across her chest. "Who could ever forget the headlines? The story went on and on. Jenny had a nervous breakdown and no one believed her, did they, Will? We were so young. We couldn't tell, could we?" The chairs stared blankly. "It was a terrible accident, wasn't it, Will?"

"It was a sad time," he pulled his woolen cap snugly over his ears.

"The fire was so hot they said nothing survived. Nothing!"

"We all saw the flames," Will nodded.

"Those boxes of fireworks." Mary said. "The tissue paper had little Chinese lanterns painted all over them. The chairs, just like these ones, were stacked up against the wall waiting for the celebrations. They said the plastic fed the fire and they burned hot, hotter than anyone's imagination could describe. When the windows burst open the fireworks lit up the sky."

Will stood and wrapped Bruno's leash around his wrist. "It's time to go home, Miss Hudson. It's getting quite cold."

"I've never run so fast in all my life." Mary felt the same heart palpitations that sent her to the hospital three months ago. "It's a terrible memory, Mr. Fortnum. They never found Colin. Not his red shirt or his new sneakers."

The sky had darkened. Wallington Park had fallen silent. The swings had stopped moving. The crows had hushed.

"He really wanted some of those fireworks." Mary held her arms so tightly she felt her joints crack.

Will covered his mouth with his hand and coughed. "Who could forget?" He tapped his pipe against the arm of the white plastic chair and the embers glowed as they fell to the ground.

"It's good to talk to you, Mr. Fortnum. There's only you and me left that remembers. It's a heavy burden to carry."

Will pulled Bruno to his side. "Come boy," he said softly. "You need to be on your way, Miss Hudson. It will be dark soon."

"The chairs, Mr. Fortnum?"

"I'll attend to the chairs in the morning."

Carlton's Blessed Toes

Carlton Commons celebrated his thirtieth birthday with a visit to his mother. "Why?" he asked. "Why weren't the extra toes removed when I was a baby?"

And his mother replied, just as she had done on each of his other birthdays. "I saw it as a sign, a gift from heaven. You are special, Carlton. From the day you were born, you were special." Her rosary trembled. "I want you to promise me you'll always embrace your toes."

He hugged his mother and hid from her the fact that the memories he harbored of school children teasing him had not diminished with time. He never knew his father, and his mother wept whenever he mentioned his name. "Too sad, too sad," she whispered into her handkerchief. So Carlton conjured a rich history about his father just for himself, a brave soldier, a wealthy businessman, a school teacher in Africa. But he never thought to ask if his father had also had six toes on each foot.

Carlton's big toes were large and spatulate, and those he admired. They kept him balanced and upright. His pinky toes, such an absurd word, were small and slim and straight. But the four toes in between concerned him. He covered his feet with wool socks in winter and cotton socks in summer, and if he wore sandals he chose sandals that concealed his toes.

One day the large toe on his right foot became painful. He could see that the sharp edge of his toenail was biting into the flesh; the skin was swollen and tender. He put on his brown Oxford and winced at the pain. He called his mother for advice.

"You need a podiatrist, Carlton." Her voice was wheezy from walking the flight of steps to Madison Street after early mass. "Look in the yellow pages." Carlton worried about his mother and that steep flight of stairs, but his mother's day began by attending daily mass. What sins she had to confess were beyond his imaginings.

In the yellow pages, Carlton found a Dr. Leonard Critchlaw not far from where he worked and made an appointment for that same afternoon. As a respected paralegal for Smyth and Guiles Law Office, Carlton was able to finish work early, so he tidied his desk and switched off his desk lamp. He told the office manager, a young women with sad eyes, he had an appointment and limped out the front door.

Carlton's problem was a minor one. Dr. Critchlaw cut off the offending piece of nail, swabbed it with a strong-smelling disinfectant and placed a wisp of cotton wool where it hurt. "You need a regular pedicure," he said. He wrote a name on the back of his business card and Carlton wondered why his twelve toes passed Dr. Critchlaw's gaze without comment.

"Marjorie's Pedicure. Appointment Required." Carlton made an appointment for two weeks from that day. At home, he soaked his foot and tended the swollen flesh, and by the time his pedicure was due the skin on his great toe was healed. The fear of showing his feet again to a perfect stranger made his pulse race. He might be laughed at; he might be refused service; he might have to explain yet again why his mother had not had his extra toes removed at birth.

But Dr. Critchlaw had advised him, and so he found himself outside the green-shuttered windows of 54 Hart Street. Marjorie of "Marjorie's Pedicure" was a woman of rounded proportions with a soft double-chin and bright gray eyes. While she gathered her equipment, Carlton shed his socks, sat up on the padded seat and placed his feet in the tub of warm, bubbling water. He sighed. He spread his toes and let the water fill the spaces; he wriggled his big toes and arched his feet, one by one. There was a hint of lavender in the towels piled beside him.

"Are you comfortable, Mr. Commons?" Marjorie draped a thick white towel over her broad lap. She peered into the tub and Carlton flinched briefly. She had seen his toes and, he was sure, had silently counted them. "Let's enjoy this, shall we?" Marjorie said.

Carlton presented his right foot. Marjorie swaddled it in her warm towel and gently patted and dried every toe. "Six," she breathed. "How perfect."

She made no further comment. Carlton relaxed. She had seen his toes and found his feet were perfect. He closed his eyes and as she tenderly patted and rubbed his feet he had a great urge to sleep. The salt rub was followed by a lotion smelling faintly of lemon. His skin tingled. Marjorie prepared each toe methodically, snipping and smoothing, plucking and stroking. For once, his extra toes were a gift and the sensation of blissful relaxation was wonderfully prolonged.

"Finished," Marjorie said softly.

He was jerked into the present. "Will you come again in three weeks?" Marjorie's eyes were bright, her cheeks flushed. Strands of hair had escaped their clip and framed her face. Carlton smiled and pulled on his socks and brown Oxfords. He was surprised by his feelings. He wanted to leap up and hug this woman. It was quite out of character, quite out of the ordinary. He had never hugged a woman, other than his mother, his entire life.

"You really need a pedicure every three weeks so your nails don't create a problem," Marjorie said. Her voice was husky and warm.

Carlton stretched his shoulders. His feet felt soft and clean to the bone. He couldn't believe how relaxed he felt, how tended. "Three weeks," he said and offered his credit card. "How wonderfully pleasant this is," Carlton faltered. His thoughts were in turmoil. "How wonderfully pleasant," he repeated and walked out the door.

During his second visit he allowed Marjorie to add a neck massage and a manicure. On his third visit, Marjorie suggested a pillow behind his head and Carlton happily breathed in the scent of lavender. She placed a warm cloth on his forehead. His half-hour appointment had expanded to two hours. His twelve toes tingled for days after each visit.

"Perfect, perfect," Marjorie murmured as she worked on his feet. She began the habit of pulling on each toe as she worked. From large to small, she pulled and stroked, and Carlton decided if heaven was filled with pedicures he'd accompany his mother to daily mass.

"How did you find me?" Marjorie asked on his fourth visit when he was settled and a warm towel was nestled around his neck.

"Why, Dr. Critchlaw gave me your number." Carlton adjusted the pillow at his back. His feet lay in the bubbling bath. "I had never had a pedicure before."

Marjorie reached down and removed her soft brown shoes. "That's interesting," she said. "Dr. Critchlaw has also tended my feet."

Carlton saw her socks had bright red diamonds woven into the wool and he watched as she removed them. Her ankles were trim; her feet were long and white. And much to his surprise, Marjorie, too, had six toes on each foot. Carlton sighed with relief and joy. His mother's words echoed in his ears. His toes were, indeed, a gift from heaven.

Marjorie pointed to the seat beside his. Carlton nodded in a blur of incredulity. She climbed up beside Carlton and slipped her feet into the bath beside his. They sat together, hip touching hip, content to inhale the soothing scent of lavender, their twenty-four toes floating comfortably together in the fragrant bath.

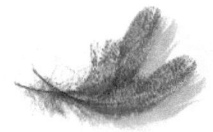

The Celebration

"Goat's in the well!" Babs McKinnon ran through the pergola and into the shed where her husband was working. "The goat, Bert, it's going to drown!" The bag of pegs tied round her waist slapped on her hip.

Bert McKinnon was cleaning eggs with a lump of steel wool. He rubbed the debris from the egg in his hand and placed it calmly in the egg-crate. "What are you talking about, Babs?" He reached for another egg.

"You've got to do something, Bert," his wife ordered. "The little brown one, Coco, she's in the well."

"In the well?" The steel wool kept doing its job.

"One minute it's eating the grass near me, next it's gone." Babs rolled her hands in her apron. "I've got wet clothes to peg out, sheets waiting, you'd better come quick." Luckily, it was the small back well, only about twenty feet deep and the water five feet or so beneath the log covering.

"Must've left the trapdoor open when I put down the beer," Bert mused. He'd finished corking the bottles early that morning. He'd put the beer in a burlap bag and lowered the round dozen into the well so it would cool nicely, ready for some late afternoon refreshment.

"Bert," she demanded. "That's our drinking water she's splashing round in."

"Alright, Babs, alright," Bert said. "I'll call Colin up to help." With that he put the egg crate aside. At the end of the yard Colin was working on the Allis Chalmers tractor. Only his legs showed as he leaned deep into the dark places of the engine.

"Colin!" Bert called. "Goat's in the well."

"What the blazes?" Colin's head emerged, red-faced from exertion. He wiped his hands on a piece of Bert's old pajamas.

"She's still splashing, Colin. We don't want the water messed with." Bert moved the wheelbarrow closer to the wall and searched until he found the hoe with a curved blade.

"I'll get some rope." The younger man dashed for the little shed. "You keep an eye on her. See she doesn't drown."

Babs led the way back through the pergola where the climbing vines held the wooden posts upright and the old carpet snake dozed in the sun. "Hurry, Bert." She was breathing hard from excitement. What a story she'd have to tell the ladies when next they met for quilting. She imagined the church hall and the row of faces turned toward her.

Bert strode behind her swinging the hoe. "You ready for a swim?" he asked as Colin arrived with the rope trailing behind him.

Babs wondered if the wooden trapdoor was wide enough to drop Colin through and she was glad Colin was young and that Bert was in charge.

"A swim? You've gotta be kidding," Colin said. "Water's freezing."

Bert took the rope and made a large noose. They could hear the goat splashing, the rasping breaths. "She's tiring." Bert tightened the knot and made sure the rope pulled through easily. "Move out of the light, Babs," he ordered.

Babs stepped back. The clothesline behind her sagged with the weight of the wet clothes already pegged out. She moved away from one of Bert's undershirts and caught the slap of a wet pants leg on her cheek.

Bert and Colin lay down on the logs and peered through the opening. They saw the goat in the half-light, hooves thrashing, head strained back. In the corner of the well the burlap bag holding the beer bottles bobbed in the wake. Bert flung the lasso toward the goat's head but the animal turned and the rope slipped into the water. "Damnation!" Bert pulled back the rope and refashioned the noose. He tried again and the same thing happened. The goat shook off the noose.

"Too far away," he said.

Babs watched her husband's hands as they worked the rope. His fingers had thickened. She saw the scabs on his left hand where the chisel had slipped a week ago and gouged the skin. She remembered how it bled and the business of getting the bandage right so it stayed.

"It's heading for the beer." Colin pulled at Bert's sleeve. Sure enough the goat had seen the burlap bag and was moving toward it. "What if he eats the burlap?" Colin asked.

"Can't lose the beer," Bert said. It was some of the best he'd made using the new hops, and he certainly wasn't going to lose it all to a little goat.

Wasn't that just like her husband? Babs thought. Being more concerned with the new hops and his latest brew than he was about the safety of the goat? Still, she enjoyed that cold beer at the end of the day. She could understand his thinking.

Bert gauged the distance from the logs to the water, then from the goat to the burlap bag. He looked at Colin's legs splayed out on the logs, his bare ankles and loosely laced boots. "Tell you what, Colin, I have a plan." If he held Colin's legs and lowered him into the well, Colin should reach the goat easily. "You drag the noose over her head and legs. We'll pull her out, no problem." He rubbed his hands on his pants. "You ready, Colin?"

Babs looked at her husband admiringly. "Lovely," she whispered. Bert was not a big man, but he was strong from farming all his life, and she trusted him. She watched as he knelt on the boards and rolled up his sleeves.

Colin looked unsure. The goat's splashing sounded weaker. He glanced at Babs who gave him an encouraging nod. "You can do it, Colin, I know you can." Colin had worked on the farm going on ten years now and she and Bert depended on his wiry strength and good will.

"Come on, now, give me your ankles." Bert reached out his large hands. "Babs, tie this end of the rope to the tree there."

Colin slid around on the logs, took up the length of rope with its large noose, and slowly eased himself through the opening to where the water looked dark and cold.

Bert grabbed his bare ankles and the edge of the trapdoor dug into Colin's chest, then into his belly.

"You'd better hold tight, Bert," Colin called. He swung slightly and maneuvered closer to the goat. Colin threw the noose over the goat's head and as the goat tried to swim away the noose slid down its neck and dropped over its front legs. The goat gave a startled bleat.

Colin tightened the noose around the goat's chest. "Done," he called. "Pull me up."

Babs saw Bert take the weight of Colin's body. She saw him dig his heels into the boards and heave but Colin's feet were slick with sweat. His hands slid down the ankles and as he tightened his grip, Colin's boots slid off his feet and flew over Bert's shoulder.

Babs gasped. "Oh, no!"

"Sorry Colin," Bert yelled as he came down hard on the logs. The rope twanged taut. There was an almighty splash and the clink of bottles.

Babs shrieked. She leaned into the well. "Colin?" Her voice echoed off the water. "Are you there?" She turned to Bert. "You should have held on," she berated Bert. "He could drown down there."

"Don't worry Babs, Colin's okay," Bert reassured her. "He knows how to swim."

"Oh, Bert," Babs twisted her hands together and rolled them into her apron. "You always know what to do."

"Swim to the beer," Bert yelled. "That's your safest bet." He reached for the hoe. If he could just get the hook into the waist of Colin's pants he could keep him afloat. He saw Colin splashing toward the burlap where he gripped the bag and hung on.

"Have you tied the bag tight, Bert?" Babs asked, her voice quivering with emotion. All would be lost if the burlap gave way under Colin's weight.

"Tightest knot this side of the valley," Bert answered. "Beer's safe, Colin's safe, now we gotta get the goat up first. Give me a hand, Babs."

Babs was used to lifting baskets of wet clothes, shifting bags of wheat for the chickens. She set herself behind her husband and took hold of the rope.

Together they hauled the goat out of the water and up through the opening. The little goat lay on the logs, soaked and exhausted, bleating mournfully. "Rub her down," Bert said. "She'll be chilled through."

Babs grabbed a towel from the wash basket and rubbed the goat's body briskly. "There, there," she murmured as the goat kicked and scrambled to its feet.

"It's bloody cold down here," Colin called. "Get me out 'fore I freeze to death."

Bert gathered up the wet rope and swung it down and over to Colin's waiting hand. In minutes, Colin's head appeared and Bert and Babs hauled him out onto the damp logs.

"You were wonderful," Babs said, handing Colin a large damp towel from her wash basket. "And Bert," she looked at his broad back and lost the words she wanted to say. "It's been a perfect day."

They didn't wait for the sun to set before trying the new batch of beer. Bert pulled the burlap bag up and closed the trapdoor securely. He undid the wet ties and opened the bag. The bottles clinked. None were broken. Babs sat between the two men on the edge of the well while the little goat grazed nearby. Bert had been right about the new hops, thought Babs, the chilled beer tasted like pure nectar prepared by a benign and benevolent god.

ℑ Machine Like ℕo Other

Susan married Geoffrey Moore in the Registry Office one Saturday morning in a new pine-green coat. It was an impulsive decision. Susan's friends were having babies and she knew her biological clock was ticking, so along with Geoffrey's warm smile and his golden retriever, Ollie, she was swept off her sensible feet. Their courtship was conducted between Susan's shopping dates and luncheons with her mother. Since her father had died, Susan and her mother, Beatrice, had been close companions.

"We're such good pals," Beatrice said as she dried the last of the dishes. "We will still be pals, Susie, won't we?" Beatrice came for supper in Susan's new house on Mondays when Geoffrey worked late at his office. Beatrice liked her new son-in-law and his dog, but she wondered why Susan had wanted to marry at all. "Why now?" she had asked Susan, folding the damp tea towel neatly over the railing by the stove.

"He makes me smile," Susan said. "And I love Ollie."

"Smile?" Beatrice paused in her sweeping. "What does that mean?" The broom caught Ollie's tail and he leapt up and skittered out of the kitchen. "You *know* I like dogs," her mother added, small lines tightening her mouth. "But dog hair," Beatrice swept briskly around Ollie's large stuffed bed, "is everywhere!"

Susan's mother felt a compulsion to sweep her daughter's floors and straighten the six cream canisters near the stove. She liked the sugar to be first, followed by the tea, not the other way around. She neatened the bookshelves, all spines upright, which made Geoffrey nervous.

"Why can't she leave my books alone," he muttered as he shuffled books, paperbacks on one shelf, hardbacks on the top. His golf magazines sat in a tidy pile on the lower shelf.

Geoffrey wondered whether Susan might be spending so much time with her mother she was neglecting Ollie. "He shouldn't spend all day alone," Geoffrey complained when he came home and found Ollie had overturned the wastebasket in the bedroom and was chewing on a discarded toothpaste tube. "It creates bad habits."

Susan could see the mess made by Ollie so she brought out the old vacuum cleaner and, though the suction was poor, she persevered until the bedroom floor was clean. Slowly, slowly, up had come the tissues, the dog hair, the toenail clippings.

One Monday evening after she and her mother had finished the dishes, they retired to the living room to sip coffee. Beatrice placed her feet on the hassock. "We can still do things together, can't we, Susie?" As an only child Susan loved the intimacy her mother demanded, the exchange of ideas, the mixing of scarves and jewelry, the many luncheons they shared. She knew her mother was finding this adjustment difficult, her marriage irksome, and that she didn't really approve of a dog on the living room carpets. Her mother liked neatness above all else, and color coordination among pillows and curtains.

For Susan's thirtieth birthday, Beatrice wanted a celebration, a meaningful memory, a week in Paris. "Geoffrey will be in Washington that week," her mother said. "Imagine, Susie. The most beautiful city in the world! You can't celebrate your special day here with Geoffrey gone."

So the week before her birthday Susan and Geoffrey ate at their favorite little Italian restaurant and made plans for Ollie to stay in Pets Haven for the week while she and her mother were away in France. "This is not like Paris," Geoffrey said extending an arm to encompass the table where they sat and all the tables beyond. "I just can't compete with your mother." And Susan packed his travel bag for Washington with extra care.

It was April, when prices in Paris were low and the weather was wretched. On her birthday the Eiffel Tower was buried in fog and Notre Dame was filled with police and reporters after a French politician committed suicide at its altar. Susan huddled under her raincoat and wondered miserably when the weather would clear. "You give up too easily," Beatrice said. "*Tres bon*," she called to anyone who happened to pause beside her, a tourist map flapping in her hand. Susan clenched her teeth when her mother practiced her fragmentary French in the tourist bus. "*Merci, merci*," Beatrice repeated with a smile, "*Bon jour*," over and over again, hands fluttering and Susan was surprised by her irritation.

Two weeks after they returned from Paris, Susan and her mother lunched together at a small restaurant called Petit Paris, and Susan voiced her thoughts about starting a family. "Geoffrey and I have been talking, mother," Susan said. "My clock is ticking. It's time for us to make a decision."

"Really, Susie," Beatrice held a salted chicken leg to her lips. "You don't want to be tied down with dirty diapers, do you? Not now, surely?" Her mother wiped specks of chicken from around her mouth. "We have so many places to see, dear. And the Bermuda cruise?" Her mother paused and looked out through the restaurant window as though she heard ocean waves lapping beyond its walls.

"But mother," Susie began. "I think it's time. Geoffrey thinks it's time."

Beatrice sniffed gently. "You're still so young, Susie. There's so much more to experience." She wiped the corners of her mouth with the red and white checked napkin.

Susan finished her chicken salad. Why hadn't she defended herself more vigorously? Until now she had consulted her mother about all decisions concerning her life, but now she had Geoffrey to talk to in the evening, Geoffrey who held her hand. It was their decision to make. Starting a family sounded perfectly sensible when they were in their queen-sized bed, together under its green coverlet.

"You have Ollie." In Petit Paris her mother estimated the tip and counted out change. "At least you can leave the dog at the kennel when we go away." She gathered up their parcels. "A baby would be so unhappy on an ocean cruise, don't you think, dear?"

Susan looked at her mother: so serious, so demanding, so humorless. Susan loved Ollie, as did Geoffrey, but surely a baby, their baby, would bring more joy than dear Ollie did. They could always have a nanny, a live-in. One didn't have to breastfeed all the time.

Susan was standing on a kitchen chair dusting the blades on the large fan in the living room when the phone rang. It was her mother's neighbor.

"It was her heart, Susan, a massive attack. She died instantly." Sylvia Green paused. "We were having morning coffee together, dear. I'm so terribly sorry."

Susan held the phone away from her ear. The words could not be real. Why, she and her mother had lunched together only yesterday. They had a pedicure together and had chosen similar periwinkle-blue nail polish.

How could her mother allow it to happen? She always had things under such control.

Susan sank to the floor and sat on one of Ollie's toys, surprised by the sudden squeak. "Mother was fine yesterday," she said. The long-handled duster lay beside her legs.

"I'm so sorry," Sylvia Green said. "Let me call Geoffrey."

"I can't believe it's happened." Susan recited Geoffrey's work number. "Tell him to come quickly." Susan wasn't practiced in making decisions. Her mind was addled. "I don't believe it," she repeated. "I just don't."

The neighbor arrived at her door within the half hour, a frozen casserole and a posy of sweet peas in her hands. "Let me make lunch for you," she said. Sylvia Green was quick to find the bread and cheese while Susan waited in a chair, glad to have someone in charge.

Geoffrey arrived soon after. He held her and consoled her. He made all the necessary phone calls and Susan went to bed and pulled the comforter with its green-buttoned cover over her head. Ollie jumped up beside her and settled in the folds of the comforter. She rested her body against the dog's back and listened to his breathing.

Susan's life loosened around the edges after her mother died. She missed their luncheons, the sharing of Netflix mysteries, the choice of cleaning products. Every day she was flooded with questions. There were so many chicken recipes on the Internet and Geoffrey was only half-hearted in responding to her questions. The green-lidded urn sitting in the center of the mantelpiece held her mother's ashes, a reminder that her mother remained in the center of her living space. She had to *move on* as the latest self-help book instructed; she had to change patterns of thinking, of habits. She and Geoffrey began to talk again about having a baby.

Two months after her mother's passing she opened the newspaper and poured her morning coffee. Ollie sat at her feet and the sun shone through the kitchen window. On page five a bold advertisement caught her eye: *A Machine like No Other, guaranteed to change your life.* It seemed like the perfect promise. She immediately called the number.

When Geoffrey came home from work she told him about the machine. "The old one has no power," she said. "We need a new vacuum cleaner."

"Whatever you'd like," Geoffrey said. He opened his newspaper and patted Ollie's head. "I think it's a splendid idea."

The day the box arrived, Susan dragged the machine out of its foam packing and allowed the dark hose to snake across the carpet. She lifted the nozzle and marveled at its lightness. Ever so gently, with the toe of her sneaker, she pressed the red on/off button and was rewarded by the husky, deep roar of the engine.

Susan looked around the living room. Ollie's toys were there beside a pair of socks and a dressing gown cord that Geoffrey had dropped. She aimed the metal nozzle at the dog's toys and with a series of *thunks* heard them rattle and squeak down the hose. She sucked up the socks, the dressing gown cord, and a crumpled take-out Starbucks coffee cup. She sucked up the newspaper, and when the sports section blocked the hose, she found a long-handled wooden spoon and unstuck the wad. *Thunk, thunk.* The sound was immensely satisfying.

She held the warm nozzle of the machine and surveyed the stripped down living room as Ollie sidled into the room looking for a treat. His tail swung past the nozzle's end and Susan heard the slithery sucking sound before he leapt to safety, a frantic scrambling of his front paws. Thank goodness she had responded quickly or dear Ollie may have gone the way of his toys.

Susan's mother had helped choose the sofa, had insisted the color was right, the cushions perfect. Without thinking it through, Susan heard a loud *thunk* and the green floral sofa was gone. She hauled the machine up the stairs to the bedroom where it sucked off the green-striped Jacobean wallpaper in long wrenching strips. She watched the pale green coverlet disappear down the nozzle and felt triumphant. The mat that once lined the hall in her mother's house and now sat under the little desk by the window was ugly. She knew it had to disappear along with the framed prints of the Eiffel Tower, her mother's memories of their Paris trip hanging on her wall. She aimed the nozzle. The mat and prints disappeared. The walls looked beautifully bare. Susan realized the capacity of the vacuum cleaner grew with use.

Downstairs again, there was still one place Susan had not swept clear. She aimed the nozzle of the vacuum cleaner at the squat green urn on the mantelpiece while she glanced out the window at the birdfeeders her mother disliked. She clearly heard her mother's voice, "Such a mess, Susie, and the squirrels!" When she looked at the mantelpiece again the urn was gone, along with the three little Dresden figures her mother had prized and the linen doilies the figures sat on. The shelf was clear except for the brass candlesticks, a wedding gift from Geoffrey's co-workers, still with their unlit cream candles. She turned the vacuum cleaner off, allowed the cord to retract into its hot silver body, and placed it carefully in the broom closet.

Susan pulled out a kitchen stool and sat, settling her new jeans on the padded cushion. Tight stretchy jeans, unlike the ones she wore to Paris. Her mother would not approve of them.

71

Geoffrey, however, had thought them perfect. With a fresh cup of coffee in her hand, Susan was surprised by her feelings: not of regret, but of missed opportunities. Where had the years gone? What had been lost?

She tore up the brochures describing the European River Cruise and pulled out her address book. She had only two friends listed among doctors and dentists, travel agents and hairdressers. Both friends had babies now and houses filled with bassinets and strollers. She would call them both and embrace the future. She had so many questions to ask them, so much planning to do. While Ollie snored happily at her feet, she picked up the phone and punched in their numbers.

The Wake

The metal ends of her mother's kitchen chair had dug two deep holes in the linoleum. "Not good," thought Elizabeth. The holes looked like two dark eyes staring up at her.

Elizabeth went to the kitchen drawer and pulled out the silver duct tape and scissors. She tore the tape apart with a quick pull between her teeth. She placed one, then two pieces of tape over the holes. With a marker, she drew two bright blue eyes on the silver tape and then drew a face around those holes like the face she planned to draw on the outside wall of the house.

Elizabeth was holding her mother's chair, ready to carry it off to the basement when Mrs. Glen entered the room. Their next door neighbor was a nosy old busybody. "What you doing, Bessie?" Mrs. Glen asked. Like she'd tell snoopy old Granny Glen what was going on. She hadn't heard the doorbell she'd been so taken up with tape and scissors and staring eyes.

"Why, Mrs. Glen, it's good to see you." Elizabeth set down the chair.

"And what do you do for a guest, Bessie?"

Elizabeth gestured for her neighbor to sit. Mrs. Glen set her plumpness firmly on the chair seat. She crossed her arms and held her elbows.

"Wait," Elizabeth said. "I'll put on the kettle. It must be morning tea time." Elizabeth had lost all sense of time. She looked at her wrist but her watch was missing.

"Your mother makes the lightest sponge cakes I have ever eaten." Mrs. Glen sighed. "So many eggs and flour beaten well! And the berries, the cream! If only she had passed on the recipe, Bessie."

It was disconcerting to hear Mrs. Glen talking about her mother now.

"We ate all her cake," Elizabeth said. "Didn't you have some at the wake?"

Mrs. Glen placed her hands on the table and examined them. "How do you get rid of these dark spots, Bessie?"

Elizabeth's hands, at seventeen, were white and delicate. "Lemon," she said. "The juice of a lemon will take them out." The spots looked like little brown dots of paint. And the skin looked like brown paper, creased and folded.

"You're so helpful, Bessie," Mrs. Glen said, her voice playful. "And the tea?"

Elizabeth set out the teacups and the tin of cookies. Had Mrs. Glen noticed the duct tape on the floor? She should explain how awful it was to have eyes watching from the linoleum, when the linoleum was so old it should have been torn up long ago. One time a cockroach had hovered outside a hole in the cupboard under the sink where the lye and carbolic acid were kept. She had screamed and reached for the wooden spoon. She must remember to cover that hole with duct tape, too.

"Remember, Bessie, when you're feeling fragmented it's good to concentrate on how you walk. Heel, toe, heel, toe! It's the rhythm you need in your head, dear. Heel, toe, heel, toe!"

Elizabeth knew it was the truth. She practiced this over and over: when the head is agitated, the feet need to be regulated.

"Do you know the waltz, Bessie?"

"Mother always said I should learn to dance, heel and toe." Elizabeth stood and held out her arms. "Can you teach me, Mrs. Glen?"

Her neighbor rose from the chair. "Come," she said, arms open. "I will show you the steps, my dear: one, two, three; one two, three."

Elizabeth's feet caught the rhythm and off they waltzed, around the kitchen table, around her mother's chair, until she grew breathless. "Stop!" she cried. "My feet must stop."

"Thank you, my dear." Mrs. Glen gathered up her bag. "Remember the steps and you can dance anywhere, anytime."

Elizabeth gathered up the teacups and put them back in the cupboard, the teapot back on the shelf above the sink. She opened the tin of biscuits and took out one coconut cookie for herself.

Elizabeth hauled the ladder out from the shed and carried it across the driveway to the back of the house. She leaned it up against the west wall where the setting sun would set the colors. She would draw it big, reaching as high as she could, setting the head directly under the eaves, away from the nesting flycatchers that came every year to build on the open beams. Each year, after the hatchlings had flown, she knocked the nest apart with the long-handled broom. This year she hoped the smell of paint would not frighten the birds. She liked the high-low notes of their morning song: sad, fleeting notes that told her they would be leaving soon, *leaving soon.*

Elizabeth steadied her body against the ladder and with the white chalk she drew the head, a large oblong, pointing the chin a little so she would remember where to draw the neck. She laughed. Could she forget the neck with its wobbly flesh? Not likely. Now for the curly hair, the ears set tight to the head, the mole on the right side cheek in front of the ear. Elizabeth knew this face like she knew the call of the flycatchers as they tended their babies under her window.

She stepped back down the ladder and retrieved the black paint. The outline had to be permanent through the summer rains, so she painted over her chalk lines, extending the neck to a shoulder line. The eyes had to be large above the curve of the nose. She painted them with a big dark iris. Then she loaded the paintbrush and gave a quick flick of her wrist. The paint exploded in a wave of little dots, like undisciplined freckles, to cover the nose and cheeks. Perfect, she thought, just perfect!

"Elizabeth," the call was sharp and clear. "What are you doing?"

"I'm coming." Elizabeth climbed down the ladder. She held the brush and paint tin in her left hand. Where was her watch? It was always on her left wrist. Maybe Mrs. Glen stole it when she came for tea. Elizabeth knew about stealing things, knew it was forbidden. There were so many things to remember. And someone was always watching her, reminding her.

"You have paint on your dress, Elizabeth, what were you thinking?" It was her mother's voice. She hadn't heard her mother coming, not the sound of the car, not her feet on the gravel.

"I wanted a painting of you. I wanted..." Elizabeth tried to brush away a paint stain on her skirt and smeared it further. "Ask Mrs. Glen."

"Our neighbor's gone, Elizabeth. Mrs. Glen died last week."

Elizabeth put the tin of black paint on the ground. She'd have to carry the ladder back to the shed, then she'd have to take her mother's chair to the basement, but no, her mother would need it now. She looked at her mother and saw her eyes were brown. She would need to change the color of the eyes on the masking tape in the kitchen.

"Remember, dear, we went to Mrs. Glen's wake." Her mother's large straw hat cast a shadow across her face, concealing her dark hair. The words seemed to come from a distance, simple and reassuring. Elizabeth remembered the wake now. She remembered the lemon sponge cakes and the bowls of fruit salad, the cut glass dishes filled with whipped cream. The church hall had been filled with people, the buzz of voices overpowering her thoughts, the music making her eyes water. She didn't like the room altered, the chairs out of place, the long table filled with plates and bowls and serving spoons. There were vases of flowers, so many colors and spiky leaves. And voices, loud, loud!

"The wake was yesterday," her mother said. "We were there, Elizabeth, and you were very good."

She allowed her mother to take the paint tin from her hand and stand it at the base of the ladder. She dropped the paintbrush at her mother's feet.

"I thought you were dead, mother." Elizabeth said. She looked at the painting on the side wall of the house, the dark lines lit by the afternoon sun. It wasn't her mother she was drawing after all. It was Mrs. Glen, who had died, the neighbor she danced with, the neighbor who stole her watch. Why, she'd recognize that speckled, freckled face anywhere.

Phillip Dunstan's Bicycle

My mother's Dodge was half on the sidewalk, half in the gutter. I was driving home from soccer practice with my best friend, Bonnie, and I was bone tired. We'd heard the sound of metal on metal so I'd stepped on the brake. The wheel of a bike stuck out from under the car.

"What now?" Bonnie hauled herself out from the front seat and looked at the bike's mangled wheel. There was sweat on her forehead. "God, Jannie! You know whose bike it is?"

I thought her legs might give way and wondered what the heck I'd do then. "It shouldn't have been left in the street," I snapped. I'd had my license six months and I thought I had this driving thing down pat. "That kid!" I was out of the car. I knew whose bike it was: small, curly hair, acne. Phillip Dunstan. Eighth grader! "It's all the kid's fault!" I needed to blame someone. "Leaving it in the street like that!"

"You're going to have to explain it, Jannie. To everyone," Bonnie said. "And your dad."

My dad! He had so many rules about using the car: Don't drive until the seatbelts click, no using the cell phone, eyes always on the road. He was not going to be happy. He'd really wanted me to get my license. "Think of your mum, Jannie. It'll give her a break from taking you places."

We got back in my mother's car and reconnected our seatbelts. I backed slowly over and off the bike and I heard the nasty raw clunks of metal. Then the tangled mess of bike grew small in the rear view mirror. We were only three houses from my home but it seemed like miles as I waited to hear whether the gas tank had been ripped off or the exhaust pipe was dragging on the ground.

"You gonna tell them how it happened?" Bonnie asked.

"You think I'm dumb or something?" I'd been checking my eyebrow color for a moment in the rear mirror, just for a brief moment, and swerved, and there was the bike.

I pulled in our driveway, leaving room for my dad's Ford. "Coming in for a coke?"

We'd been friends since tenth grade, Bonnie and me. Bonnie lived two houses down on the other side of the street with an iron gate and two tall pines defining the front door. She had well-mown lawns and no gardens because her mother worked. She had an older sister who took care of things, like getting Bonnie to school on time and regulating the TV. Bonnie often came to my house to watch her favorites, like Skin Wars, so her sister could watch Chopped. I was first to get a car license, first to pluck my eyebrows, first to have a boyfriend, although Daryl and I weren't going together anymore because he took up with Lisa Davis, a stupid tenth grader.

I was locking the car door like my dad had warned me to do when I saw Phillip Dunstan's mother hurrying around the hedge, then coming up our driveway.

"Janice!" She was a little breathless.

"Yes, Mrs. Dunstan." I shoved the car keys into my pocket and straightened my shoulders.

"I saw you." When she came to a stop her pink sneakers were aimed right at me. "I saw you run over Phillip's bike. How could you leave it there?" Her voice was shrill.

"Have I done something?" I stared straight at her. Phillip was her only son, a mama's boy, and a liar. I knew he was hanging out at the pool with the senior boys after school. Maybe I could bluff her into believing it was someone else's car did it. "Lots of black Dodge cars on the road, Mrs. Dunstan."

"I was by the kitchen window and I saw you were driving." She folded her arms across her chest. Her cheeks were flushed and her bottle-blonde hair curled damply around her ears. "Where's your father? Is he home yet?"

Mrs. Dunstan gardened like crazy and expected everyone else on the street to do the same. She was into politics, too, a rabid Democrat and carried signs when elections came around, knocked on doors and handed out fliers. We were proud Republicans. She drove a Mazda. We drove American-made because my father held you should always buy local. No handouts from the government, no woman's liberation stuff, no sleeping with boys until you're married. Around election times my father stood on one side of the road and Mrs. Dunstan stood on the other, both holding signs for opposing candidates. He and Mrs. Dunstan didn't get along.

I squared my shoulders. "Phillip has to be more careful with his bike." I sighed loudly so she could hear me.

Mrs. Dunstan had regained her breath. "Janice, when will your father be home?" By the tone of her voice and the mention of my father I guessed it was probably better to apologize. I was just starting to run the words over in my mind when Bonnie, who was standing beside the car with her mouth open, blue cardigan stretched tight over her chest, spoke up. "Hello Mrs. Dunstan."

"Why, hello, Bonnie, is your mother well?"

"Mother's fine." I swear Bonnie almost curtsied. "I have to be going, Jannie," she said. "My night to make supper."

"I'll see you tomorrow then." I knew I couldn't rely on Bonnie to support me. We were all neighbors on the same street but her mother was also a Democrat like Mrs. Dunstan. When elections came around she and her sister helped Mrs. Dunstan put flyers in our mailboxes. It felt like a betrayal being reminded of that. Tomorrow I'd ask her to return my silver handbag. And my new mink-brown eye shadow.

"Look, Mrs. Dunstan, Phillip shouldn't have left his bike in the road. It's his fault, really."

"You should've been watching where you were driving, Janice." Mrs. Dunstan's voice sounded whiney. "If only Mr. Dunstan was here." Her face crumpled a little. She was shorter than my mum, petite, almost fragile in her light summer dress.

I nearly felt sorry for her, but her husband had been gone for years and according to my dad, good riddance. Mr. Dunstan was known to have a rotten temper. My dad said he wasn't worth the stamp on an envelope and stamps have never been worth much.

"Dad should be home soon," I said.

We were at a dead end. *She said, she said.* I knew from Law and Order that we wouldn't have a resolution. I was in for it. Mum would take Phillip's side. And dad? He didn't like Mrs. Dunstan, partly because she mowed her lawns every second Sunday of the month at 8:00 a.m. and my dad hated the noise. He'd go down early on those Sundays just to give her a piece of his mind. "Poor woman," he'd say when he returned. "She forgets how noisy those new machines can be." He always came home looking hot and bothered and mum, looking up from my Entertainment magazine, would wonder out loud why he couldn't let it go.

Mrs. Dunstan tapped my arm. "You'll have to pay for it, Janice. I don't have the money to buy another bike."

I wondered then who she thought she was talking to? I wasn't even getting minimum wage at the ice rink, helping kids put on their skates and cleaning the floors in the bathroom. Plus I was saving for a Goddess hair mousse that was advertised to turn straight hair into cascading ringlets. Bonnie said it was foolproof and she knew all about hair with her mum working at Cherished Curls.

"I don't have any money." I thought about crying but I was too angry to make tears. Though crying might work if Mrs. Dunstan thought I was really sorry. I just knew I had to fix this before my dad got home. "I'm really sorry," I said. "I should have been looking." That might get me off the hook for now, get past telling my dad all the details. I searched her face to see if she believed me.

"Really?" Mrs. Dunstan looked surprised.

"I'll tell my dad. He'll be home soon."

"Maybe your dad can sort this out. I don't want to bother your mum." Mrs. Dunstan looked up our driveway toward the house. "No one's home yet?"

"Six," I said. "Mum's out with her quilting group."

"Then I'll come and talk to her tomorrow, Janice." Mrs. Dunstan began walking down the driveway. She had nice legs and I liked her pink summer sneakers. Mum favored flip-flops at home. I figured Mrs. Dunstan was younger than my mum. And in better shape.

"Mrs. Dunstan," I called. "Do you know where Phillip is?" Why couldn't I let it go? Mum talks about having a generous spirit, that honey works better than vinegar, but I didn't want to put out my hard-earned money to fix Phillip's bike when it really was his fault.

She hesitated. "Yes?"

"He should be home right? His bike there and all."

"Yes." She looked puzzled. "Of course he should be home." She pushed her hair back from her forehead. It was a weary gesture. "Where could he be?"

Should I tell her now or wait? I didn't know them all but I'd bet Sam Morgan was one of the older boys he'd gone off with and I hated Sam. "He's probably with Sam Morgan. You know him?" He was a senior, too, like me and the biggest pest on earth. Always teasing, "Hey, fat girl," he'd call to me, call to anyone, with a toss of his blonde hair. He knew how much that hurt. All we girls hated him and his truck with the loud twin exhausts.

Peggy Dunstan looked defeated. First the bike and now she'd found out her son was sneaking out with scrappy boys who might be bad news for him. Should I tell her where I thought he'd gone? I hoisted my backpack up my shoulder. "He's probably down at the pool with the older kids."

At that moment my father pulled into the driveway. He stepped out of the car and slammed the door. "What's happening here?" He didn't sound happy. "Janice? What's going on?" My father likes peace when he gets home from work. He sits with his feet up in his Lazy Boy and says, "Give me a little space, a cold beer, and don't pester me until I've read the newspaper."

He turned to our neighbor. "Peggy?"

Peggy? She was always Mrs. Dunstan when he spoke of her at home.

Mrs. Dunstan pulled a Kleenex from her sleeve and wiped her eyes. "It's best if Janice tells you."

"Janice?" My dad was waiting. I could see he was tired. He had his briefcase in his hand and a newspaper under his arm.

There was no sense in lying to him so I explained. "Phillip left his bike on the road and I drove over it."

My father took Mrs. Dunstan's arm. "I'm sure it was an accident, Peggy."

Mrs. Dunstan wiped her eyes. "Oh, Ryan," she said. "You know I can't afford to buy another bike."

Ryan? She called my father *Ryan?*

She blew her nose gently and looked up at him with wet eyes.

My father's face was flushed. He leaned toward her, too close, like he might hug her or something. *Hug her?* I didn't recognize these people.

"You go in, Janice, wait for your mother," he said. "I'll take Peggy home."

Take Peggy home? Like they were old friends? And what was with her, *Oh, Ryan?* My mind was racing. What about being one of those damned Democrats? And one of those damned neighbors who abuse the noise laws on a Sunday morning?

My father put his arm around Mrs. Dunstan's shoulders as they walked down our driveway. He was tall beside her and she was shorter than my mum but with better legs. They were walking slowly and Mrs. Dunstan was talking. As I watched she leaned against my father and their hips bumped. I picked up his briefcase and newspaper and fumbled my way into the house.

Mushroom Soup

Constable Bradley keeps knocking on the front door. "The neighbors called, Chrissie. Are you alright?"

Through the keyhole I see his gun is holstered and his hands are hooked in his belt. He has a kind smile. Not that I trust him, but I know I've got to answer his questions. He came once, no twice, in the last year to settle us down after one of my agitations. He's nice enough, but more my parents' age than mine.

Today is Monday and I remember I prepared Sunday lunch yesterday. I open the door.

"Your neighbor says he hasn't seen your parents," Constable Bradley says. "Hard to believe, Chrissie, they're not in the garden in this nice weather."

He looks around the kitchen, past the table and chairs to my rug frame. I realize I'm still holding my hook. The wooden handle feels smooth in the palm of my hand, like the rounded cap of a mushroom. The mushroom soup is still on the stove. My father collects the lovely little morels from under the apple trees in our back orchard.

"You hooking a new rug, Chrissie?"

When I set the rug on my frame, the basket of cut wool at my side, the morning passes. Sometimes I forget lunch when I'm hooking a rug, with the cat crying to go outside fit to wake the dead. I like the sun coming in the kitchen windows and the scarlet geraniums right there where the petals light up like drops of blood. They're my geraniums, started from cuttings a neighbor gave me years ago. Mother doesn't like them, "Scraggly things," she says. "Scraggly weeds, really." I won't have her telling me that anymore. I'll move them to the windowsill in my bedroom so I can see them when I wake up mornings. My kitty can sit in the sun beside them.

My cat is smoky-blue, a wild little thing. Lives outside most times and only comes in when it rains because she doesn't like the thunder, hides under my mother's chair and mother says, "Pull her out, Chrissie, put her outside!" I don't want to do that, with the lightning and all: she could be struck down. I want her with me all the time so I'll hook my kitty's likeness into the rug. I have my mother's old winter coat on the kitchen table. The coat is blue-and-gray checked and roomy enough. I've cut the coat into strips with mother's large-handled scissors and it looks like fur once it's hooked.

"Chrissie?" Constable Bradley picks up the pieces of my mother's plaid coat. "Tell me what happened here."

Mother's blue coat is so right for my kitty-cat rug. The background, now, I'll have to think about. Charcoal perhaps, with streaks of red. My father's wedding suit was charcoal and the pants' legs are still quite usable. The red, well, mother had a red wool scarf. "You need some color," mother told me. I wasn't much into color before I started hooking. "You need something to do," my father said, "instead of pacing." He was right and I knew it but it always made me mad when he lectured me. Pacing settles me, settles the agitation. And hooking does too.

Constable Bradley points toward the verandah. "Maybe we should sit outside."

How can I settle down? I thought the mushrooms were perfect, always were, nestled in that rotting tree stump at the bottom of the orchard. Apple trees give up the best morels, and my father collects them in season. He has a little knife with a short curved blade. "Perfect for morels," he'd say to me while I carried the basket. "Do stand still, Chrissie." I waited in my shoes and socks, Sunday dress, all very neat. Mother prepared the morels for Sunday dinner along with whatever vegetables come from the back garden. And chicken, roasted like always.

My kitty cat leaps up on the kitchen counter. I pick her up for a stroking. My parents don't like the idea of me having the cat inside. They say she has fleas that infest the house. "Get that cat out!" my father says. "Or I'll drown it!" What does he know about cats, calling them vermin, and my mother fussing about fur on her chair pads. I can have my kitty sleep on my bed if I want.

It will take my new hooked rug for itself, in my bedroom alongside the geraniums.

Constable Bradley is speaking to me. "You need to come, Chrissie, sit for a time." He hasn't gone. I'd left him while I was getting a pot of tea but he must have gone through the rest of the house. He's come into the kitchen and he's standing behind me. I was boiling the water and there was the rug I was figuring, my cat drawn on it, and mother's coat stripped and ready. Now the kettle's singing and he's here in the kitchen with me.

He unplugs the kettle and pours the water into the teapot. Black tea. None of this green tea that mother talks about. I mean if it's so good we'd be growing it here and not in some foreign country. I move the pot of mushroom soup along the counter to make room for the tea tray, mugs and sugar, no milk.

Constable Bradley holds the tea tray steady as we pass through the doorway of the dining room. I smell rotten apples in the air. "We'll have this tea on the verandah now," he says. I follow his broad back as he walks by the dining table. He steps neatly around my father's feet, the linen serviette still tucked in his collar, and my mother's feet, caught up in the crocheted rug she favored, which had snagged a little on the large bunion on her right foot. He's crowding me, moving me quickly through the French doors. "Mind where you step," he says. The cat in my arms purrs against my cheek: a comfort like always.

"Come and sit down, Chrissie. We don't have to rush." We are on the verandah and Constable Bradley pours from the brown teapot.

I know there's ways of answering so I have to choose my words. Our chairs face the vegetable garden and I can see I need to pick the last tomatoes before they rot. Do I tell him I made the soup? Or that I was the one who collected the black morels because father's bursitis flared up? In the kitchen I split them with a carving knife and the center was pulpy, not hollow like good morels should be. I needed to think which trees I'd collected them from, I needed to go back out to the orchard for more morels, but father was calling. "It's nearly noon, Chrissie. Are you getting our lunch?" He's always calling, always impatient. I want them to be quiet, to leave me to my rug hooking and my kitty cat.

Constable Bradley moves his chair to face me. "Your parents are dead, Chrissie. You need to tell me what happened." He is very serious. I know I have to tell him what I did but I want to go back into the kitchen and finish my rug. I have to move the geraniums. And clear the dining room.

I have to pace. The *rattley* jangle in my head sends my feet tap-tapping. I circle the small table where the morning paper lies unopened, pause at the steps leading down to the barrel of yellow-orange nasturtiums. I know what's happening. I'm agitated again. I snip some dead leaves off the potted begonia plants mother keeps on the verandah rail. The cat is still in my arms and purrs against my neck.

"Come and sit down, Chrissie," he says again. He offers me the mug with the little orange cat on it, my favorite. I reach to take it and the hot tea slops on my wrist.

"Not now." I can hear my mother's voice: *How many times do I have to tell you, Chrissie! Stop the pacing! Settle down!*

Constable Bradley leans forward in the rocking chair. "Come and sit, Chrissie," he says quietly, pulling the second chair closer.

I hold the cat too tight and it digs its claws into my shoulder. There will be blood drops on my white blouse. What if I forget about them and put my best blouse through the hot wash, seal the blood in? I move the cat to my other shoulder and count the slats running down from the verandah rails: fifteen slats between the support posts and four posts to the end where the mandevilla vine climbs freely.

Constable Bradley rises from his chair. "Chrissie," he takes my arm. "I need you to talk to me."

I had cut the mushrooms down the center like my father taught me and inspected the inside of each morel. I wanted to be helpful. Time was running out. I told mother I would fry them up, make some soup for lunch. "That's nice of you, Chrissie," she'd said. Her sewing machine went *thumpety-thump.* "Not too much butter, now." She was making a dress for me, sewing it on the old treadle machine, *thumpety-thump,* on and on. "Come and get fitted," she called, expecting I'd drop whatever I was doing. Father flicked his paper the way he does when he gets impatient.

I continued to fry the onions, added the morels with the pulpy centers, the chopped-up parsley, a half teaspoon of ginger and cayenne and poured in the chicken broth. I served lunch at noon. Was it yesterday noon or the day before?

"Thank you, Chrissie," mother said as I ladled out the soup.

Father picked up his spoon, "Today, you've been very helpful, Chrissie." I gave them the large white napkins that mother kept for special occasions. Father tucked his into his shirt collar. "Aren't you having some, Chrissie?" father asked.

"Not today," I said.

On the verandah, there are forty-five slats on our side of the steps, another forty-five beyond the steps, eight posts in all, plus the two posts supporting the front steps. I feel my kitty cat purring on my shoulder. When mother had guests she often served homemade shortbread.

"We ate the last of the shortbread," I say, remembering my manners. "Would you like some soup and crackers with your tea?"

"That's very thoughtful of you Chrissie." Constable Bradley cups his mug and leans back against the cushions.

I like that he is quiet. I put the cat down on the vacant chair. "It's no problem, Constable Bradley. This mushroom soup is one of mother's favorite recipes."

"Thank you, Chrissie," he says, crossing one boot over the other. "While we eat, we'll talk, you and me."

As the Wind Blows

Robbie Crowe was having an early evening drink with his best friend Charles at the Irish pub on Tremont Street, the quiet time between happy hour and when the serious clientele arrived. They had worked together in the same accountancy firm for several years, and they were talking about the Red Sox and whether the present lineup had a chance this season with a young pitcher and some new batting talent. They were arguing as friends do when a woman walked in and joined them. She was short and curvy with long sparkling earrings and an easy smile.

Robbie waited as Charles introduced her. "This is my new recruit, Sarah." She extended her hand and Robbie held it. Her nails were long and glossy. She explained how she was still learning the routines of the office but enjoying the work. "I like working with numbers," she said with a smile. "They're so safe, so wonderfully predictable."

Robbie liked the color of her lips, the way her hair dipped on her forehead. "Are you an accountant, too?" she asked Robbie.

"Not anymore. Once I worked alongside Charles. Now I wash windows on high-rise buildings."

"On high-rise buildings? Isn't that dangerous?" Sarah's eyes widened. "I've got a thing about heights."

"He loves it," Charles laughed. "But it was kinda sudden, right Robbie?"

Robbie picked up the story. "I was sitting at my desk covered with files and empty coffee cups when I looked up. There was a guy standing outside the office window." Robbie took a sip of beer. "He seemed suspended in air. The clouds looked like spun sugar and gulls flew around his feet. He was out there alone and no one noticed."

"But you saw him," Sarah said.

"Okay," Charles said. "You two look happy. I'm off." He finished his drink, put on his coat and said, "See you tomorrow!"

"Ciao!" Sarah said. "He's a nice boss," she said as she turned back to Robbie. She sipped her drink. "So, Robbie Crowe, seeing that window washer changed your life."

Robbie watched the tiny beer bubbles explode inside his glass. "People don't really see me when I'm working. They don't hear the sound of my squeegee, the song in the cables." Her earrings caught the light as she turned her head. "Do you ever see the window washer on your building?" he asked.

"Never," she said.

"No one really sees us out there and I like that." Robbie signaled for another beer. "From some buildings I can see the harbor way off, the ships."

"What about the wind?" Sarah asked. "Isn't that dangerous?"

"It's my job," he said. "I love it."

Robbie had been trained by the best window washing crew in Boston. He knew the perfect amount of soap to use. He'd practiced the zigzag swirl of the squeegee, the upward flick of his wrist so water didn't drip on the windows below.

"We only use Dove soap," Robbie said with a smile.

"Dove? Like I use to wash dishes?"

"Odd, isn't it?" Robbie sipped his beer. "We share something in common."

Sarah moved her bracelets up and down her wrist. "I work on the fourteenth floor and I've heard the wind out there. It sounds pretty scary."

"It's like being inside an orchestra." He paused. "I used to play bass guitar in high school and I had this gift. I could hear the individual instruments. On stage I was alone and the lights blocked out the room, just like the sun blots out everything beyond the window. I rarely notice the rooms beyond the glass."

Sarah gave a little shiver. "But isn't it scary out there on your own?"

"I don't think about it." Robbie saw the look on her face. "There's a safety button I push if the wind gets too strong," his voice was reassuring. "It sends the cradle to the roof, simple as that."

"Cradle?"

"It's called a cradle. The thing I stand in. And sometimes it rocks."

"A cradle, like what a baby sleeps in?"

Robbie moved his hand in a see-saw motion. "You ever see that film about the French tightrope walker?" Robbie asked. "He and some friends strung a wire between the Twin Towers? The people down on the street couldn't see the wire so they thought he was walking on air."

"What happened?"

"Way up there he did a somersault." In his mind's eye Robbie saw the tiny figure on the wire holding the thin line of the pole for balance. "Can you imagine that?"

"He must have been very brave," Sarah said.

Her hands were smooth and her nails were painted a delicate pink. The old bricks on some of the buildings had that same pinkish tone. When his job took him into a calm evening, the sun's rays set those bricks on fire. "Are you free next Friday?" he asked.

Robbie and Sarah met the next week at the Irish pub during happy hour.

"How long have you been washing windows?" Sarah adjusted her silver bracelets and they caught the light. Robbie thought of piccolos and saw tiny flying notes.

"Three years."

"Three?" Sarah raised her glass. "If you're a Pisces or a Cancer, three is lucky." She smiled. "I'm into astrology."

"I'm a Gemini." Horoscopes didn't really interest him but Sarah did.

"Of course you'd love the job, you belong in air." Sarah patted Robbie's arm. "I'm an Aquarius, and Gemini and Aquarius get along great." She ran her hand through her hair. "I do Tarot readings on the weekends."

Robbie had never had a Tarot reading but once when he was at a 4H Fair a gray-haired woman in a bright shawl offered to do a reading for him. She'd spread the cards and he saw a skeleton and a knight on his horse and a man hanging upside down. The old-fashioned pictures had unsettled him. "Not now," he'd told her.

If Sarah believed in the cards, he didn't want to disappoint her.

"What you do sounds interesting," Sarah said. "You know the kid's nursery rhyme, the lullaby? *When the wind blows the cradle will rock*. Being an Aquarius, I get to stress over things. It worries me, your cradle rocking."

"You get used to the wind." Robbie moved the salted peanuts around the bowl. "Everything changes with the wind, the time of day, what month it is, what part of town I'm working." He flipped a peanut into his mouth.

"I guess it's all perfectly safe if you know what you're doing." Sarah brushed her dark hair off her face.

"It's not always perfect. Not when a pigeon comes and sits on the cradle." He laughed and brushed salt from his hands. "Messy things, pigeons."

"You're a Gemini," Sarah lifted her glass in an informal salute. "And I'm an Aquarius. Both air signs. The stars are aligned." She settled the bracelets neatly on her wrist. "If you're free this weekend, Robbie, would you let me read your cards?"

They'd only been married two months when Robbie found Sarah seated at their kitchen table holding her Tarot cards. The lamp lit the side of her face and sharpened her cheekbones. Three cards were spread before her, a True Love reading: the eight golden cups, the wheel of fortune, and the fool; all were cards he knew showed change and uncertainty.

She glanced up at Robbie, worry lines pulling her brows together. "Every time I do this spread, one of these cards turns up."

"Just probabilities," Robbie said. He prodded his swollen cheek and felt the welt where a wasp had stung him that afternoon. He realized Sarah was waiting. "The cards?" he said. "It's all accidental."

"You've never taken the Tarot seriously." Sarah gathered up the cards. "Ever since we met you've only pretended to believe."

"Don't you remember? It was you who said we were made for each other, Gemini and Aquarius?"

Sarah put the deck away in its velvet bag. "Nothing's clear anymore," she said, pushing away Robbie's hand as he reached for her.

On the weekend while they were having breakfast and the early sun poured in through the kitchen window, Sarah told Robbie she was having dreams that woke her, disturbing dreams she couldn't remember clearly once she was awake.

"It's the change of season," Robbie assured her. "At work I see pollen floating round me like a mist. It's got to be around at night." Robbie finished his pancake. "I bet it affects our breathing so we don't sleep as well."

That night Sarah woke Robbie. She was crying. "They're not strong enough," she repeated. "I'm afraid the cables will break." He held her and wiped the perspiration from her forehead. He kissed her damp cheeks.

"Those cables are strong," he said. "Sometimes the wind simply plays them like harps."

"Harps?" she shivered. "Did you hear what you just said?"

How could he get her to understand? "There are different wind sounds, Sarah. If you could just be up there with me, you'd hear what I hear."

One Friday while Robbie was setting the table for supper he heard the neighbors' kids playing kickball out in the street. It was a dangerous time, early evening, when motorists were tired, not driving carefully. It was more dangerous playing in the street at night than working up in his cradle during the day. He was glad they didn't have kids to worry about or Sarah would be stressing out about that, too.

"Come up with me," he said to Sarah as they faced each other over the kitchen table. Maybe if she went up with him on one of the smaller buildings, when there was no wind, she'd understand.

"Are you crazy? I can stand on a corner of Tremont Street and listen to the wind. With my feet on the ground!" The steak and onions gave off a tantalizing smell. The food was singing, sizzling. Normally he loved that sound at suppertime.

"Maybe we could do it at your office." He noticed she'd pinned up her hair with the two silver hairclips he'd given her on her birthday. "Cleaning the windows on your high-rise would feel like I'm halfway to heaven. It's straightforward work; the window ledges are narrow and the brick work is even." He reached for his knife and fork.

"Stop talking of heaven and harps. I need a break from worrying about you."

The steak looked perfect, covered with browned onions. The fries looked like lengths of caramel candy, evenly browned and crunchy.

"Thanks, love," he said. "Smells good." Washing windows made him hungry. He started to cut the steak and his right arm ached. He used a strip of rubber, pulled across his chest, to strengthen his shoulders and rotator cuffs, to keep everything from stiffening up. Every morning he did stretches and bends to strengthen his knees.

Robbie cut up the last of his steak. Hadn't he explained already how the sun's heat baked the bugs on the cement between the bricks like tiny gems? That there were no spiders up there, no webs catching dew? That sometimes a host of lacewings got caught in an updraft of air and floated past his hand like tiny parachutes. "It's the pigeons on the ledges, Sarah, that are the most fun."

"I hate pigeons," she said. "They're lice covered. There has to be lice all over those bricks."

He gathered the fried onion on his fork. "Good maintenance, Sarah, is a way to honor the brickies and glaziers who've worked so hard." He thought of all the men who'd worked on the buildings through the years and how he felt a responsibility to maintain them.

But Sarah was not listening. "I've read the Tarot, Robbie. You know how reliable the Three Card Spread is. They're not happy about us." It was the tone of her voice, the stillness of her hands that caught his attention. "I'm not sleeping enough and I'm groggy all day. Yesterday, Charles asked if everything was okay." She folded her arms. "How do you think that makes me feel?"

"What made him ask that?"

"I tripped." Sarah leaned back in the chair. "I fell into Marcy's chair and knocked all her stuff off the desk. You can imagine what people were saying behind my back. Someone asked was I pregnant? I had to explain I wasn't sleeping because of the nightmares and Charles said maybe I needed a holiday."

"Tell Charles to mind his own business." Robbie dipped a piece of steak into the meaty juice. "You knew what I did when we got married, Sarah. You were fascinated by the idea that I was a Gemini and you were an Aquarius. You said we were made for each other."

Sarah wiped her mouth on her napkin. "After I tripped, someone leaned in and smelled my breath. Can you imagine?" Sarah flicked the napkin in Robbie's face. "I said, 'What's going on?' And he said, 'Just checking.'"

Robbie mopped up the last of the juice with his bread. "I thought we'd sorted this out. This worry you have about my job." He couldn't stop the anger in his voice. He had a sudden image of himself scrubbing the pigeons' muck off the brick ledges. No wonder his arms ached.

Sarah slid back her chair. "You don't listen."

"Wait, Sarah. There must be a way to figure this out. Maybe

you should read the cards again." They should have been mellow, maybe watched a little TV and spent time cuddled on the couch. He realized they hadn't done that together in some time. Sarah was too tired, she had some work to finish, had to wash her hair.

Sarah gathered up the plates and dropped them in the sink. He leaned against the door frame as she scrubbed and rinsed them.

"We've had this conversation before," he said. "And we worked through it. Surely we can do it again."

"Not this time." She put the ketchup bottle in the refrigerator and slammed the door. "I did the six card spread and it showed we were living different paths. That we weren't synchronized." She wiped down the counter. "Can't you come back to the firm, Robbie, to a desk where it's safe?"

"You know I can't." Robbie should have told her months ago he didn't believe in the cards. How could he say anything now? "You know I'm careful out there. You know I test the equipment before I use it."

"I just can't take the stress, Robbie." Sarah turned her wedding ring around. "Those cables give me nightmares!"

Robbie thought Sarah had come to terms with the cables and the wind. Maybe her nightmares were about something else she couldn't talk about. "What's really bothering you, Sarah?" He felt the need to shake her so the truth spilled out. He trapped his hands under his armpits. "Has something happened at work?" He couldn't believe she would leave him over his job. There were ways of getting past nightmares. Army people did it all the time. Meditation. Breathing. All sorts of stuff he'd heard about on TV. "You could try yoga," Robbie said finally. "Maybe relaxation would help."

"Yoga?" Sarah snorted. "That's your answer?" She walked out of the kitchen and slammed the bedroom door.

Within six months their divorce was finalized. Robbie wasn't ready for a new life. It had all happened so fast. He thought of resigning from the company and moving out to the suburbs, but he loved the tall office buildings in the city. He was having breakfast and planning his work schedule when he got the call to clean windows at 137 Tremont. He knew that address and he knew Sarah still worked in that building. He gathered up his tool bag, folded in extra socks and a warm jacket. He made a cheese and pesto sandwich, whole wheat bread, and pulled on his Red Sox cap. He checked out his living room window for wind and cloud formation.

He arrived at the Tremont Street building and went to the roof. Setting up his gear, he lowered the cradle until he was positioned outside her office window on the fourteenth floor. He swung gently in his cradle, the bucket of soapy water at his feet. Sarah looked up at the window and Robbie waved, but he knew the sun's reflection hid him from view. He worked steadily, the task made easier when clouds suddenly covered the sun. He could see Sarah clearly: her dark pony tail, her crisp white blouse. She was stapling papers together and he saw she was still wearing their engagement ring but on her right hand.

He wanted to call, "Look up, Sarah! I'm here. I haven't left yet!"

The wind soughed through the cables, low and moaning, oboes and tubas. The cradle rocked sharply, the bucket tilted, and water splashed on his boots. He'd been so busy watching Sarah, willing her to look up, to see him, that he'd lost sight of the clouds. The cables twanged like bass guitars. A strong gust of wind blew the cradle away from the building. One moment the squeegee was in his hand, the next moment it had been torn away.

The clouds darkened the sun further and the glass disappeared. Sarah looked up and saw him. Robbie saw her mouth open in astonishment.

The first large raindrops hit his jacket and the wind's intensity picked up further. He pressed the UP button but it didn't respond. The cradle flew out and back like a child's carnival ride. Once, twice, it hit the side of the building and brick dust flew into his eyes. He fell to his knees. He stabbed the UP button again. This time the cables responded, those good, strong cables he trusted with his life. Sarah disappeared from his sight, first her pale legs, then her white blouse, and finally her dark hair. He gripped the sides of the cradle as it rose while the wind played in the cables like a chorus of heavenly harps.

The Little Fox

I raised my arms, lifted my right foot a few inches off the floor and braced my body against air. This was my fourth yoga lesson, and though I tried to concentrate, all I could think about were the little netsuke figures that were missing, gone from the corner chest in front of me. There had been five of them, gifts my father gave me when I was a child. He brought them back from his trips to Japan: a little tortoise, old master Baku, a rabbit, a dragon, and the little bushy-tailed fox. They were all precious to me, and now the rabbit and the fox were gone. I had no idea when it happened or where they might be. This past weekend I thought to dust them and found the figures were missing, that there were only three instead of the usual five.

I breathed in slowly, centering my thoughts to keep my balance.

"It takes practice," Madelaine repeated. My yoga teacher held her thin arms over her head and stretched. The dark hair framing her face fit like a soft helmet. "The head," she continued, "needs to reach for heaven." Her fingers pointing to the ceiling lightly touched each other. There was no slack in her arms; no tell-tale flap of skin above her elbows. I wondered if with practice the skin under my neck would miraculously tighten. I raised my face to the newly washed living room window and noticed that a spider's web crisscrossing the outside corner had captured a struggling insect.

When Madelaine first came to the house my husband was with me in the kitchen. He watched as she leaned her bike against the garage wall. "This girl," he had paused, "This is your yoga teacher?" I had asked her for lessons to trim down, to surprise my husband, to gain serenity and get my younger body back. "She needs a good meal," he said. "At least three times a day!"

She came to the back door while I was stacking breakfast plates in the dishwasher. Sally, our golden retriever, barked inside the screen door. One of the boys, in his rush for the school bus, had spilled milky cereal on the tiled floor and when I straightened from wiping it up, I saw her through my husband's eyes. She looked younger than when she spoke at the local Library in a flowing top and dramatic makeup. She had spoken passionately about "maintaining serenity in a chaotic world," and I was at that place in my life when I needed to believe change was possible.

"Breathe," Madelaine coaxed as we stood on our yoga mats. "Breathe deeply."

I settled my hips and positioned my feet. My calves felt tight and the toes in my left foot numb. She had given me a mantra in my first session: "My body is beautiful; my mind serene." I filled my lungs and straightened my shoulders.

"So," she continued. "One is aligned." Madelaine's spine was a steel rod. Behind her was the mahogany chest where the five netsuke figures had been kept. My father had explained they were special gifts to mark the birthdays he had missed. Through the years they sat in the shadow of the table lamp next to my mother's small pewter jug. He had explained how the netsuke secured the little pouches and medicine boxes hanging from a gentleman's sash. "Because the kimono has no pockets," he had explained. "They're a counterweight to balance the men's boxes and money pouches." I had cupped each one in my hands, given them names, placed them on different chests and windowsills through the years, until we moved into this house and I put them on the mahogany chest in our living room.

Madelaine placed the sole of her right foot against the inside of her left knee.

I copied her pose and felt my right hip click. I brought my hands to my waist to steady myself and a cough rose in my throat. Madelaine was in my house to teach me how to cultivate the serene life. When she spoke at the library she made it seem possible to live serenely in my chaotic world with two young boys, a work-addicted husband, and an undisciplined dog. I thought improving my posture would settle my mind, that being an athlete as a teenager would transfer to my middle-aged body. She easily convinced me that gentle yoga was the answer. "Six sessions and I can teach in your home," she said.

I had hesitated. "In my home?"

"No problem," she said. "I like teaching in my client's houses." She had continued with a smile, "I can bring my mat. And water. One on one is nicer than in a group." It seemed easier for me to tumble into loose clothes and not drive somewhere, so I agreed.

Madelaine transferred her weight from one foot to the other. She held her pose, tall and thin in her black leotards, her body a perpendicular stroke against the living room window. I held the back of the sofa and tried to breathe evenly.

"We need to rest." Madelaine sank down on the living room rug and assumed the Lotus position. She closed her eyes while I settled on a large cushion and folded my legs. "Ten minutes," she said softly.

I glanced at my watch. These ten minute rest periods seemed an eternity. I started a grocery list in my head and thought about the many things I had to do later that week, one boy to the dentist, the other to softball games. Madelaine's big soft bag lay on the sofa, slumped against the cushions. It seemed empty. My little netsuke figures were made from polished tagua nut. Each time my father had arrived home from a business trip he had brought a small black lacquered box and nestled in the white silk was a little wooden figure.

Old Baku, my father had told me, "Eats nightmares so he will keep your dreams safe," and I had hugged him. The tortoise, which was not much larger than my thumb, symbolized long life. The dragon was to remind me to be strong and generous. And then he had brought a little brown rabbit. "It will be your good friend," and I had immediately named it Hazel. The last figure he had brought home before he died was the little fox that sat on its haunches and seemed to watch my every move. "The fox is a trickster," he had warned when he brought it for my ninth birthday, and I had kept the red silk ribbon that bound the gift box.

"Stillness," Madelaine broke in to my thoughts, "must be practiced every day." She drew in a deep breath and exhaled slowly through her pursed lips. "Every day you must perform ten breathing exercises." She stretched out on the rug and lay on her back. "The abdomen holds the yellow chakra." She raised her buttocks off the floor. "Lift," she said and held the pose, her eyes fixed on the ceiling light. Her feet, I noticed for the first time, needed a long soak in a hot bath.

"Relax your body," she said. "Breathe."

I stretched out on my mat and pulled my abdominal muscles tight. I had questioned the boys about the missing figures. "No," they had said. "Why would we take them? They came from Grandpa." The boys had played with them through the years, had made up their own stories, slipped them under their pillows as sleeping buddies. My husband had asked them, "Who's been to the house? Who had friends visiting who might have snagged them?" Snagged? Why that word? Stockings got snagged, my hair got snagged on unruly shrubs while I raked leaves in October; the word had a distinctly alien feel. Had Madelaine snagged the little figures?

I brought my knees to my chest.

"Ten times," she counted, "one, two, three...." Sally started barking to go out. This happened every lesson. She had been out earlier, and I wondered if she had another infection, which meant more medication while my husband held her jaws open and I threw the tablet onto the back of her tongue.

"Stillness comes," Madelaine repeated, "when your mind clears and your thoughts are refined."

"I have to let Sally out," I said. Madelaine turned on her side to face me, the mahogany chest a backdrop against her body.

"You seem tense today." Her face was tinged with irritation. The first time Madelaine had come to the house, she explained that dogs upset her equilibrium, her serenity. So Sally had to stay in the laundry while Madelaine was there.

"I just have to let Sally out," I assured her. "I'll only be a second." How, I wondered, did I agree to this?

Madelaine moved into the Lotus pose.

"Sorry," I called as I held Sally's collar and led her out the door, where she could run in the fenced-off backyard.

The day Madelaine had arrived for my first lesson she had looked around the kitchen and poked her head into the living room. "Can I set up in here?" Her big fabric bag hung from her shoulder and a yoga mat poked out from under her arm. She tossed her bag down on the sofa and scanned the room. She pointed to the window. "Beautiful," she said. "I love crabapple trees." It was mid-June and the tree was covered with white blossoms. She threw out her arms to embrace the room. "This is lovely. And those?" she said, pointing at the netsuke figures. "Are they antiques?"

Of course they weren't. My father had bought them for a child. But seeing her obvious delight in my house, I didn't want to disappoint the young yoga teacher who rode her bike to people's houses. "Probably," I said. "My father found them in Japan years ago."

Once Sally was settled back in the laundry room, I returned to the living room where Madelaine was still in the Lotus pose. Her big old bag remained against the sofa cushions. What should I say? *Madelaine, dear, when did you take my netsuke figures?* I glanced at the mahogany chest. Five netsuke figures sat next to the pewter jug. Five? I couldn't believe it. They were all there. The tortoise in front of old Baku, the dragon and the rabbit, and the little fox sitting slyly behind them both.

I avoided Madelaine's gaze by focusing on the window. The blossoms on the crabapple tree were luminous. The sun fully revealed the tangle of branches. In a matter of days the blossoms would be gone to be replaced by clusters of red berries and ugly dark grackles.

"Are you alright?" Madelaine asked. "Is the dog okay?"

"Why did you take them?" I held the back of the sofa and pointed at the figures on the mahogany chest. "The two little animals?"

"You noticed?" Madelaine stretched her arms over her head. "I only borrowed them. Really."

"They were gifts from my father."

Madelaine stood and began rolling up her mat. "I guess this is our last lesson." She wrapped a piece of cording around her mat.

"Why did you take them?" I waited for an apology but Madelaine was absorbed in tying the cording into a bow. "And then return them?" Couldn't she see how wrong it was?

"I thought they might be worth something." Madelaine tucked the yoga mat under her arm. "Being antiques from Japan."

"Did you think I wouldn't notice?"

"They were so small." Madelaine glanced around the room. Her gaze settled on a framed Matisse print of the Blue Nude. "I've come four times and you've never asked me about myself." She shrugged. "And you never thought to pay ahead."

"At the library, you said to pay at the end." I heard the patient voice I used with the boys.

"Anyway," she looked around the room. "You have so much. I didn't think you'd notice they were missing." She looked younger than when we first met at the library five weeks ago, her face clear of makeup and earrings.

"It was terribly wrong of you." I wondered who had done the larger wrong, me boasting about the netsuke's worth or Madelaine who thought they were valuable and took them.

"My rent was due and I have medical bills." Madelaine's voice rose. "It seemed an easy way to make some money, that's all." Her cheeks were flushed. "You can pay for the four sessions and I'll get going." Her arms were crossed; she was no longer my yoga teacher, serene and at peace, but a thin young woman who needed three square meals a day.

I paid her in cash. I didn't want her to see my signature or know which bank we used. The twenty-dollar bills were creased and worn, and they were quickly transferred from my wallet to her outstretched hand and then into her shoulder bag. There

111

were no goodbyes or best wishes. From the kitchen window I watched her mount her bike and set off down our driveway. I listened to Sally's barking from the laundry room and knew the boys would be home shortly, full of stories and grubby knees. In the mornings, when the house was quiet, I would practice serenity alone and trust that Baku would eat my guilty dreams.

Blue Dog Mask

Didi was fifteen and longing for change. One week she stayed with her dad on tree-lined Lemon Street and one week she stayed with her mom on Barnes Avenue down by the dry cleaning plant. She was not very organized so she left clothes in one house, shoes in another, school books spread between them. On Friday nights and weekends she stayed with her Gran in a little condo filled with religious icons and a blue-robed Virgin Mary hanging on the wall behind her bed. Gran lit a candle every Sunday for her granddaughter. "Jesus listens," Gran told her, so Didi prayed for friends and for Carl, smooth-skinned and dark-eyed, to notice her. So when Libby and Elspeth invited her to hang out with them it seemed like her prayers had been answered.

"You want to have some fun Friday night?" Elspeth asked. The ends of Elspeth's braids were bleached. Her sequined top spelled Madonna.

"Better than watching old movies with your Gran," Libby added, a big purple bag hanging from her shoulder. The two girls stood arm in arm, waiting for Didi's reply. They wore loose tops over sparkly tights and silver hoop earrings. Didi didn't have any tights and she never wore earrings.

"I'm coming," Didi told them. Then she told her Gran she was going to Elspeth's to study for a science exam. They were learning about the human body: muscles and bones, and all the stuff that made Miss Doherty blush when the boys sniggered: long names like gastrointestinal and duodenal and fallopian.

"See you tonight then," Libby whispered, with a poke in Didi's back during class. Didi sat up straight and fiddled with her ballpoint, Hudson Eye Care in gold lettering on the side. She gave Libby a secret thumbs up. Didi had brought a change of clothes in her backpack, the new top with the skinny straps and a short black skirt. A tube of blue eye shadow. Elspeth said she had everything else.

Didi knew Jimmy Frist would be there with his friend Carl. She'd seen Carl one Saturday smoking behind the Odeon. His father had opened the Cobblers Emporium last year and Carl's clothes smelled of oiled leather. Didi was reminded of horses and saddles and rich people on TV. He was nice though, and when he didn't have a cold sore his lips were nice, curved and soft. She'd be able to talk to Carl about leather boots and jackets with fringes.

The bell rang for the end of class, and Didi hefted her backpack. Two more classes and then they'd be off. Mr. Bronson taught art. "Today, we'll do papier-mâché." There were piles of newspapers, pots of white glue, brushes and paint tins on his desk. Didi wondered where all the newspapers came from, who could read so many?

"Today," Mr. Bronson spoke over the screech of chairs, the slap of books, "We're making animal masks." He brought out a mound of wire armatures each shaped loosely like the head of a large dog, without ears and with stubby jaws.

"Shit," Libby whispered. "Mucky stuff and glue. Hate it."

They began tearing the newspapers up. The ripping sound put Didi's teeth on edge. She stacked the strips and Elspeth stirred the glue. Libby held the armature at arm's length. "It's large enough to fit one of our heads," she said. "We could make a Halloween mask."

"Sure." Elspeth was arty. She pushed Didi aside and quickly brushed glue on the paper strips and molded them over the frame. Didi watched as the wire disappeared and the head took shape.

"The eyes," Didi asked. "What do we do for eyes?"

"Paint them on," Libby said, "with curvy eyelashes." Libby leaned back in her chair and picked at a hangnail.

Mr. Bronson hovered over each table, making suggestions, redirecting the boys who started to slap glue on each other's hands. Didi could hear Jimmy Frist's voice, "I...am...your... father." Low and menacing like Darth Vader.

"Do we need a tongue?"

Didi stirred the paint tins, blue and red. "A tongue would be good," she said, but no one heard her.

"Make it a blue dog," Libby cut in. "How about you, Didi, you want a blue dog mask for Halloween next week?"

Didi thought Halloween was silly. She knew the high school kids roamed in packs down the back streets tossing toilet paper over trees and smashing pumpkins while she stayed at the condo and gave out treats. She wondered what it might be like to do bad things one night a year, not mean things but silly pranks that didn't hurt anyone.

Elspeth drew in two slanted eyes above the nostrils. "Paint them red," she said, handing Didi a brush.

115

Libby placed her hands inside the head and held it firmly while Didi brushed over the damp newspaper. The blue was a violent blue, not periwinkle like her new sweater but a blue that smacked of badness and defiance. She worked paint under the red eyes and some dripped onto Libby's wrists.

"Clumsy, Didi," Libby wiped the paint off with furious dabs.

"I'm sorry, Libby, really I am."

Elspeth took the brush from Didi and moved her to the side. "I'll finish the eyes." And Elspeth painted in dark pupils and long curling eyelashes.

Libby shoved the head into Didi's face. "Woof, woof!" she barked, and Didi recoiled. It was large enough to fit over someone's head.

"Cut the teasing." Elspeth took the head and placed it on the table, stabilizing it with paint pots. "We'll come back when it dries." Didi washed her hands at the sink.

Libby swung her backpack up and flicked hair from her face. She got Jimmy's attention four desks over and when he looked up she mouthed, "See you later." He pointed at them, and Libby raised three fingers. Jimmy nodded and pumped fists with Carl standing beside him.

Didi looked at the dark blue head. Could it be her Halloween mask? Its eyes glowed under their seductive lashes; the jaws were parted and the snout looked blunt and ugly. She wondered if a red tongue between its jaws would have changed it somehow, softened the look, maybe made it look a little less threatening.

"You coming, Didi?" Libby called.

Libby sprawled on the bed while Elspeth opened a makeup box like something Didi had seen on HGTV. It was filled with tubes and bottles and brushes. "Here," Elspeth said. She pushed Didi toward the mirror. "Take off your glasses and close your eyes."

Next year Didi was going to have contacts, no more nerdy glasses. Didi wished it had happened already.

It took a full half hour to get her face looking the way her friends wanted her to look. Didi's eyes were larger and darker, and with lipstick her mouth was wide and full. She hadn't noticed her cheekbones before, and how the little bones at the base of her neck cast shadows. Elspeth brushed out Didi's pony tail so her hair fell to her shoulders. Didi had thick blonde hair and Gran had told her it was her crowning glory.

She looked like herself but more so, more defined, brighter. Even her pink top looked different with Elspeth's strand of glittery beads and earrings to match. She ran her hands down her hips, over her flat stomach. Her last year's black skirt was tight. She'd only brought black flats while Libby and Elspeth wore heels, but Elspeth said that wasn't important. "You can borrow one of my diamante hair clips to hold your hair back," she said.

"Where are we meeting the boys?" Didi put on her glasses and looked in the mirror. If Gran saw her now she'd hardly recognize her. She saw herself as Carl would see her tonight, like one of the cool girls.

Libby giggled. She held up the papier-mâché head and barked, "Woof!"

"Funny, funny," Elspeth said. "Bring it along, we'll show it to the guys."

Libby put the dog's head in a canvas bag.

They walked down the street, arm in arm, like friends. It was only three blocks from Elspeth's house, under streetlights and past whitewashed fences. The tennis courts on the corner were lit up and on one of the courts, a game was in progress. Didi heard the smack of the ball, the sliding of tennis shoes across the clay, the sharp volley of men's voices. The streetlights glowed and the leaves on the box trees glittered with promise. They passed behind the tennis pavilion and there between the trees was a small shed where the tennis equipment was stored. In the semi-darkness, Libby opened the door.

"Come on, Didi," she said. Elspeth gave her a little push.

Didi didn't expect the room to be so small and dark. It smelled of oil and leather, cigarettes and sweat.

"You here already?" It was Jimmy's voice. There was a scramble of shoes and a cigarette lighter flashed. "We just got here," Carl said from across the room.

"Where'd you put the candles?" Jimmy wore a blue sweatshirt and his face was flushed. "Time to party."

Didi smelled beer. She saw lumps of netting and pillowy cushions on the floor. They were using a wooden crate as a table and on it were half a dozen beer bottles, a saucer ashtray.

"And look who's here!" Jimmy said holding out his arms. "The beautiful Didi!"

Carl patted the cushion beside his. "Come and sit."

"Candles someone?" Jimmy lit a cigarette.

Elspeth reached into a cupboard by the door and produced two wine bottles holding candles already packed with melted wax. "Light them up," she said.

"Guess what we have?" Libby opened her canvas bag. "Didi made a dog mask for Halloween." Libby held the dog's head high. In the soft candle light the blue darkened to black and the red eyes glowed.

"Halloweeeeeen!" Jimmy pulled out the word, long and soft. "Wear it, Didi, be a sport." His hair was curly black. He reached for her hand and a broken nail scratched her palm. She pulled away and Jimmy made faces at Libby, snarling and woofing. "Let's see you wear it, Didi, be a little bitch dog for me tonight."

Didi felt the blush. These were boys from class. She knew them, knew they could be silly, just like Gran said. She could leave anytime if she wanted to. She could walk home on her own, just four blocks in the opposite direction from Elspeth's. The heat in the little room made her nauseous.

"Not nice." Elspeth picked up a cigarette. Her face was shadowed. "Got a light, Jimmy?"

Didi thought she was going to fall and reached out a hand. Carl leapt to his feet and placed two hands on her waist. "Cut it out, Jimmy," he said. He gave a little *woof* and blew on her cheek. "Is Jimmy scaring you?" He smelled of leather oil and peppermints.

Peppermints. Her Gran sucked peppermints to ward off colds. She looked at Jimmy's flushed face, at Carl's forced smile. She saw the canker scab on Carl's upper lip, the tease in his eyes. Gran was right; these boys were young and silly and playing at being grownup.

Libby still held the blue dog mask above her head. "Come on Didi, don't be a spoilsport. It will look great."

Carl's hands tightened on her waist. "Trick or treat?" he whispered, his mouth close to her ear.

"Try it out, Didi," Elspeth said, "See if it fits." A thin stream of cigarette smoke spiraled up from her nose.

Didi reached up and pulled the mask out of Libby's hands. She looked at the horrid blue head, the eyes that leaked red paint, the foolish eyelashes. She tossed it into Elspeth's lap and pushed Carl's hands away.

"I'm going home," Didi said. She put Elspeth's necklace and earrings on the table and the diamante clip from her hair. "I don't need them," she said.

"Wait a minute," Carl said, "You leaving already?" He held out a bottle of beer. "I thought you and me were going to party."

"No Halloween doggie?" Jimmy drawled from his cushion, "Come on Didi, don't be a spoilsport."

Libby shook the dog's head in the air. "Going home to Gran, Didi, see some old movies?"

"Not nice," Elspeth called. "Waste of time."

Didi walked up the path. The air smelled fresh, smelled of wood smoke and fallen leaves. The tennis match was still underway and the men's voices were clear and lighthearted. Before she reached home, before Gran saw her, she'd put her school clothes back on and wash her face. If Gran wanted to watch a movie, well, then, she'd keep her company and they'd share a bag of hot popcorn together. Growing up could wait for another day.

A Glass of Ale

I joined Maeve Morstan at Harpoon, the local beer palace, for a late lunch. We sat on the bench outside the back window, basking in the pale afternoon sun, two glasses of ale on the table between us along with paper plates and crushed napkins. Her crutches leaned against the brick wall, her plastic shopping bag was on the seat of the wheelchair I'd brought along for the trip home. I had been a community nurse in Branson for two years and had forged a friendship with seventy-five-year-old Maeve after her right leg was amputated. Every week I checked to see she was up and about, that her stump was healthy, her other foot a good color, her toenails clipped.

We soaked up the sun. I was in shorts and Maeve had her skirt pulled up so the puckered skin of her stump was exposed. "Vitamin D works wonders," she said. The bag of stale bread in her lap came from Eddie, manager of Harpoon, who kept the leftover bread from lunch for Maeve and the sparrows.

"They're company, Lily," she said as she scattered the bread crumbs. "Cheeky little buggers. Come and eat!" The birds waited in the dusty oleander shrubs among neglected nests and shattered beer bottles for the rustle of her paper bag.

I admired Maeve's independence, her many friends. My work was my life. I was years older than the other community nurses and, though we worked together, I was not included in their social gatherings. Maeve was old school: she wasted nothing and wanted little. She found her clothes at the local thrift shop: men's gray trousers knotted below the knee or skirts that swayed and fluttered like empty clothes hung out to dry. I'd been on my own since I was a teenager and like Maeve I'd learned to be frugal.

"How's your hip?" I asked as Maeve settled on the seat. "Bruising better?"

Last week she'd fallen outside the supermarket. She fell on her crutches and her shopping bag had split open. "If the sidewalks were kept up, I could manage," she said when I had applied ointment to the deep welts on her thighs. "What I really need, Lily, is a motorized wheelchair. I need to be independent. I can't have everyone running round for me."

"Why don't you write to the local newspaper then?" I had suggested. "Tell them the sidewalks are terrible. Tell them they need to take care of their disabled taxpayers."

"I can't do it myself," Maeve had said. "You're the clever one, Lily, could you write it?"

Writing was not my strong suit, so I had spent hours composing the letter, rewriting, getting the commas in the right place. The letter was published in the *About Town* section. I stressed that if the town didn't do something, the writer would sue for compensation to cover the cost of a motorized wheelchair. The letters continued for weeks as readers replied about a range of town needs but had little regard for the cracked sidewalks. One writer urged Maeve to start a daily blog, but no one suggested they start a fund to buy her a motorized wheelchair.

On the bench outside Harpoon we sipped our ale in comfortable silence until Maeve stirred. "You ever marry, Lily?"

"Never met Mr. Right, Maeve."

"You know," she said, "I had a boyfriend once. He went off to Viet Nam and he never came home." Her right hand cupped her stump. "You know how you wait? Just in case someone's got the name muddled, and he arrives home and no one's there to meet him." She threw out more bread crumbs. "I've often wondered what I would've done if I'd opened the door and he was standing there." She patted my knee. "What would you have done, Lily?"

"I don't know," I said. Maeve's face was raised to mine and I saw how she might have looked fifty years ago, how her smile lit up her milky blue eyes. "I can imagine how hard that would be," I said. "Not knowing." My father had died in a car accident when I was nine and my mother had been tight-lipped when I had asked for details. Her silence had puzzled me. Two years later she died from cancer, and my aunt told me my father had been out drinking with friends. Without putting it into words, Maeve and I understood each other, we understood the business of grieving.

"His family, Maeve? Did they know about you?"

"He hadn't told. It was just between us." She raised her left hand. "I don't even have a ring to remember him by."

"I nearly got married once." I hadn't told Maeve about my boyfriend. How he had a wiry red beard that grazed my cheek. How his stack of books kept falling off the kitchen table and how he wanted to be a zoologist. "Back then," I told Maeve, "I was going down one path and he was going down another. It would never have worked."

"That's life, dear." She shook out the last of the bread crumbs and crushed the paper bag. "You can't want what you can't have."

I was living in a one room apartment, isolated from the other community nurses and looking to move. I had met some of the people in Maeve's apartment block and liked them, so I asked her to tell me when something opened up in her building.

"You'd like it here," she'd said. "We're all getting older but we take care of each other."

The sun had passed behind the tall pine tree at the edge of the lane and it was cooler now on the Harpoon bench. It was time to see Maeve home. As I brought the wheelchair alongside her, a young man appeared around the building.

"Maeve Morstan?" He had a camera strung around his neck and a canvas hat square on his head, the long ties trailing. "*The Mountain Times*," he said. "Can I get a photo?"

Maeve adjusted her skirt so her stump was hidden, and I crossed my ankles. I was conscious of the empty glasses on the table beside my shoulder bag.

"Who are you?" I asked.

"Johnson," he said. "Ray Johnson, photographer for the *Times*." He looked at Maeve, at her one leg, the old wheelchair. "You raised our readership, did you know that?" His large camera covered his face. "So many letters and all."

"No sir," Maeve said. "I didn't know that."

"We'd like to get a photo, okay?" His camera snapped.

"Photo? Front page?" Maeve patted my knee. "Better than letters, Lily, for getting the word out." She shifted on the bench and her crutches slid down the brick wall and clattered on the pavement. "Maybe this way I'll get a motorized wheelchair." Maeve beamed.

Ray Johnson cocked his head. "Motorized?" He stared at the fallen crutches, then at the old wheelchair. "What about that?"

"It's only on loan." I kicked the chair gently. "It's old and it's heavy. Maeve really needs a motorized wheelchair. She needs to be independent."

His camera clicked busily. He wanted a shot of her one leg, and was angling to get the crutches in, too. Maeve put her arm around me and leaned into my shoulder. We smiled together. After a few minutes, Ray Johnson pulled a card from his pocket and handed it to Maeve.

I picked up Maeve's crutches as he started putting bits of camera away.

"This wheelchair is important," I said. He was smaller than me, and when he looked up I found my voice. "With an eye-catching headline you could ask for donations and have the money sent care of the Branson Community Center."

"Okay." He held his bag against his chest. "I'll do my best. Check out tomorrow's edition."

"If I'd fought in the war now, Mr. Johnson," Maeve called to his retreating back. "I'd have me a new leg *and* a motorized wheelchair." She heaved herself up with the aid of her crutches. "Thank you, Lily. We've just got to hope." We started the short walk home with Maeve holding the crutches on her lap along with her bag of groceries. The path wasn't entirely smooth, and Maeve seemed to have gained some weight since last week.

"Maeve," I said as the wheelchair clattered over the pavement ruts. "You know I can't do this much longer." I stopped to catch my breath.

"I'm betting on Mr. Johnson," she said. "We'll wait for tomorrow's paper and then figure out how to use the money when it comes in."

Maeve was a born optimist. Good things seemed to happen around her. We reached the apartment block where Maeve lived. Her neighbors had recently built a ramp to the front porch and added a spring-opening device so she could open the front door more easily.

"Hello Maeve." Ben Hodges came out from behind the hedge. He wore orange gloves and carried long-handled shears. He nodded at me. "And you, Miss Lily, you well?"

I was breathing heavily. "Road's getting steeper!" At this rate I'd need to get out my jogging clothes and shape up.

Ben nudged me away. "The Barlows are back," he said to Maeve. "They'll be glad to tell you about their trip to Florida. Eddie's brown as a berry."

He and Maeve had lived in this block of apartments for twenty years. I wondered if there'd ever been more to their friendship, both living on the first floor, Ben ready to lend a hand when her sink blocked or a light bulb needed changing. He was always there when Maeve arrived home, welcoming, friendly. I felt left out.

I waited beside the ramp as Maeve told Ben about the photographer from *The Times*. "We were sitting in the sun, Lily and me, outside the Harpoon and this nice man from the newspaper came." She straightened the crutches on her lap. "And, Ben, I think he's going to get me a motorized wheelchair."

Ben pushed Maeve up the ramp and unlatched the door. "I'll take it from here, Miss Lily." He pushed Maeve over the threshold. "Really, Maeve, a fancy new wheelchair! When it arrives we'll travel the world together."

The door shut on their voices. Our friendship stopped at the door of her apartment, always had, always will. But if I lived there it would be a different story. Ben would have said, *Why, Miss Lily must come, too. She wrote the letters for you that got you the wheelchair.* And Maeve would have chimed in, *Of course Lily must come with us. I couldn't think of leaving without Lily.* And then I'd join them as we walked through the front door together.

Two Swallows

I was on my way to Celestial Heavens, the tattoo shop on Western Street, when I stopped into Wanda's for some coffee. The notice board near the door had a new postcard. It was sent by some regular customers, showing the deep rich colors of the Grand Canyon and the words *Come Back Soon* written in fancy script along the bottom edge.

"The usual, Jillian?" Wanda pushed a latte across the counter.

I pointed to the postcard. "The Barkley's having a good holiday?"

"They say it's the best!" Wanda wiped a circle of coffee off the counter and slapped the cloth over her shoulder. "See you tomorrow then?"

I pushed the door open. The coffee was hot and strong. I remembered our Grand Canyon trip when I was ten and we went there on holiday. Mother wore a blue flowered dress and a floppy white hat she'd dug out of storage. "Sun," she'd said, "have to look after your skin, Jillie." Living in Maine, we didn't take that too seriously, so I'd never owned a sunhat. Mother had packed her clothes neatly, everything folded, perfume bottle tucked into the toe of her white shoe. My father lounged on the bed, cigarette in one hand, asking, "You packed my things, babe?" I could hear the waves crashing on the sand not far from their bedroom window. The Atlantic Ocean was gray and salty, and I couldn't wait for the sun-filled adventure ahead.

Celestial Heavens: the sign was eye-catching, a fireworks display of glowing moons and stars on an azure blue background. I paused at the doorway and looked at my hands. I wanted a small tattoo that I'd see every day. I wanted to connect with who I was, where I'd been. It's the small details that come in flashes when you least expect them. Like that trip to Arizona. My bedroom at the Sunset Lodge had a woven Indian blanket. I don't know if I heard my parents' voices loud through the walls or if it was something on TV, some show about parents breaking up that became lodged in my memory.

Celestial Heavens had ribbons fluttering from the doorknob and planters of red geraniums on either side of the steps. I tossed my coffee cup into the trash can and stepped inside. The guy at the desk was gnomish, balding. "You have time to do a tattoo?" I asked.

Behind him was a leather chair, like something in a dentist's office, a table with his gear on it, a curtain pulled to the side. "There's always time." He pushed back his chair and stood. Five feet nothing, hands placed side by side on the desk, long-fingered, neatly shaped hands.

"I need a tattoo." I put down my bag. "Here," I said, pointing to the inside of my wrist. "Somewhere I can see it every day."

"Nice pale skin." He held my hand in his cool palms. "No rings?"

I shrugged. "There's plenty of time for that. Today I want something to remember the good times I've had."

"Ah," he ran his finger over my wrist. "Don't we all have those?"

"To remind me I had a family once."

"I need more than that," he said, dropping my hand. "You want to look at my art. Get some ideas." The book was slim, sharp-edged. Like the Rand McNally atlas my mother threw at my father's head as he lay on the bed in Arizona. "Done," she had shouted. "It's done."

I had an hour or two to fill, so I sat in the hard-backed chair across from his desk, no softness, no cushions. I opened the book of possible tattoos. I was thinking something simple, done in a single sitting with as little pain as possible. I'd forgotten the Ibuprofin a friend had suggested for after.

"So," he folded his hands together. "What has meaning for you?" His nails were almond-shaped and painted with pearly nail polish. It was the color inside the broken mussel shells my brother had collected on the beach, the day I caught him crying. The sounds I heard mingled with the discordant cries of the seabirds strutting at the edge of the waves. Two years apart in age, my brother and I shared everything until we didn't and by then it was too late to go back.

"A bird," I said to the tattoo artist. "On the wing."

"Give me the book." He thumbed through the pages. "Anything here you like?"

I scanned two pages of birds doing all the things that birds do. I stopped at a swallow, wings spread, tail split. "There." I pointed. "Two swallows. Isn't it true that swallows return?"

"You want two?" he asked. His left eye was a little off center. I almost regretted my decision but his hands were beautiful. I trusted those hands to create a new part of me, ink over the hard memories, perhaps force new ones.

"Yes."

"Two birds," he repeated. "Two sittings. One to outline, one to fill if you want color."

So why was I doing it? Two swallows could mean my brother and me being a family again. A tattoo is forever, unlike some families who get lost and disappear. Two days into our Grand Canyon holiday my dad announced they were splitting up. We had just come back from riding donkeys down the narrow canyon path, and my mother's white sunhat had blown off and spiraled down to the canyon floor. My brother and I stood on either side of their king-sized bed staring blindly at our mother as she zipped up her suitcase.

In Celestial Heavens, the artist took my hand and turned it this way and that. My nails needed shaping and one finger had a stab of ballpoint pen, left from putting my bag together as I rushed off this morning. My skin looked a little dry, a little scaly.

"Here?" he said. "Along the wrist?" He picked up some green latex gloves, untied the curtain and turned on the lights. "Make yourself comfortable."

My brother said once that tattoos were crass, that body art sagged in time along with the ageing skin. "Ugly," he'd snorted. "Can't even think about it!" Yet, one summer when I visited him, I saw he'd tattooed a tiny spray of blue flowers on his arm. When I asked if they were forget-me-nots, he pulled down his sleeve and turned away. I never asked again, but I wanted to believe it was a sign he, too, was wishing for a family reunion.

"Relax," the artist said as he arranged his tools. I closed my eyes as he tapped lightly over the inside of my wrist. He sketched some faint lines on my skin, set out a few dots. I felt the scratch and pulse of his tattoo gun. "Lovely," he said as he smeared petroleum jelly on my skin. His head was bent over my arm, and I saw his hair had thinned on top like my father's.

"Just black?" he asked and jiggled his machine. "I can put a little blue on the wings, make them catch the light."

Mother had a small dragon tattooed on the back of her neck. "It was done in those crazy days," she'd said. "With a little pot to ease the pain!" It was black ink only, with a curly tail and a faint puff of smoke near its nostrils. When she set her hair in a roll on top of her head, her neck was exposed. I'd run my finger over that little dragon as she sat in her chair watching her favorite TV show. I'd reach up with my small hand just above the back of the chair. That tattoo called to me.

"Just black," I said, "Black is clear, defined." The scratching continued and it felt as though he was pulling out the fine hairs, one by one. Not painful, but constant. I watched the outline of the birds emerge, their delicate wings spread, mutely following each other over the veins in my pale skin. Even now, my brother and I wondered if we'd puked once too often in the back of the car or argued too loudly when our parents were resting.

"It's done," the artist said. He put aside his tattoo gun and handed me a tube of antibiotic cream. "Keep it clean. Hot water and cream for two weeks." He waited patiently for me to claim my handbag and write a check.

My wrist felt puffy, heavy. These were forever birds. The two swallows flowed calmly up from my hand, and when I flexed my wrist they seemed to take flight.

The Empty Birdcage

I sat on the curb with my best friends, Jess and Laura, and watched the movers unpack the white moving van outside number eighty-seven Loudon Street. It was a two-story brick house surrounded by a white fence, two mailboxes down from my house. I strained to see past the flowering pear tree overhanging the footpath.

"It's going to take ages to unload all that junk." I stretched my bare legs. My sneakers scattered some pebbles and I watched a small black beetle as it clung to a blade of grass.

"Look at that sofa!" Laura whistled through the gap in her front teeth. It was covered in shiny black leather, and after the sofa there were spindly-legged chairs and polished tables and large boxes filled with unknown treasures. The two large men who did the moving ignored us. There were rolled-up carpets, cushions, beds and mattresses, small trees in big tubs. Then one of the men emerged from the van carrying an elaborate wire birdcage and a curved metal stand.

"Where's the bird?" I whispered. Who has a birdcage without a bird?

"Dead probably." Laura giggled. "The journey and all."

"Maybe it's for plants," Jess said. "I've seen them in magazines. Potted flowers and vines. They're very in."

The tall white stand had four curved legs and curly bits and knobs and a large central hook to hold the cage. It was beautiful. To have something as wonderful as a birdcage just for plants was beyond my practical world. "If it's absolutely necessary," my mother would say when I asked for a new skirt, a tartan hair ribbon, a painted eggcup. Few of my requests were *really* necessary so I had given up asking unless I could show real need.

"I think it's stupid," I said to conceal my longing.

"They have a girl our age," Jess announced as the men drove off. Her mother was president of the middle-school PTA and was the first to welcome new families to the area. "She's going to be in our class."

We sat on the curb a while longer hoping to catch sight of this mysterious figure, the new girl on the street who was our age. Laura pulled her pedal-pushers over her knees. The wind blew a few flaps of packing paper along the footpath and into a pile beside the fence. The new people would have some cleaning up to do.

On Sunday I walked down Loudon Street to meet Jess at the corner drugstore for a malted milkshake, and as I came to number eighty-seven the new girl closed her front door and walked to her front gate.

"Hello there! You've just moved in!" I called. "I saw your moving van."

"You live here?" she asked.

I pointed behind me. "Two doors up."

She wore a pearl ring on her right hand. "I see," she said as she closed the gate.

"I'm going down to the drugstore, to meet a friend," I said. "You want to come?"

"I'm catching the bus. I have to go out."

"The Hudson's didn't have any kids." I looked over at her house with its many windows. "Do you have your own bedroom?"

"Of course." She looked surprised at my question.

I shared my bedroom with Mandy, my younger sister, who was a pest most times. My mother told me she can't help it because she's only eleven. I wanted a room where the only clothes on the floor were mine, where the desk held only my books, and when I sharpened a pencil it stayed sharp until I wore it out. Miss Wilson told us in English class that, "Someday each of you will have a room of your own." Like the English writer who stuffed her pockets full of stones and waded into the river. I wondered at the time how you would know the number of stones you'd need to drown yourself.

We stood outside the gate. She was pretty, hair blonde and straight, pale skin without freckles. "I don't know your name." I said, feeling foolish beside this tall quiet girl who hadn't asked anything about me: about the street, about school, about moving here.

"Sally," she said gazing over my head. "Sally Noonis."

"I'm Frannie, short for Frances Miriam Worthing." It was a hell of a name. She looked at me and I wished I hadn't pulled on my oldest sweatshirt that morning, that I'd taken time to brush my teeth.

We walked in silence to the corner and she got on the bus. She didn't wave. She didn't say "see you tomorrow at school." She was like the wooden box with a secret opening Gram had given me at Christmas. My fingers had searched the edges, the seams in the wood, until I finally discovered the latch and the lid sprang open. The box had a red velvet lining but it was empty. "I don't know

135

what you want anymore, Frances, you're growing up so fast," Gram had said. "It's up to you to fill the box."

On Monday in English class Miss Wilson led a discussion on *Lord of the Flies*. She asked what being friends meant and what it meant to be loyal to another. No one raised their hands. She let the silence lengthen. Then hands shot up. My father once told me that very few people can withstand a long silence without speaking. It was during the discussion on friendship that Sally Noonis arrived in class and the discussion ended. Miss Wilson indicated the seat in front of me. She slid into her seat and put her bag on the floor. Of course everyone stared. She straightened her books while Miss Wilson finished her little speech of welcome.

Jess collared Sally at lunch. Jess was a softball player and used to chasing things down. "Sit with us," she said. "We all live on Loudon Street now."

"Nice." Sally spoke without inflection. She didn't acknowledge that we'd spoken already. She had her sandwich neatly folded in greaseproof paper, inside a plastic bag, then in a brown paper bag, and finally in her backpack. That was a lot of wrapping for a single egg sandwich. She also had an apple and a container of yogurt, strawberry by the look of it. And she had a spoon, not a plastic one like we always brought, but a proper piece of flatware.

"Do you have a bird?" Laura asked. Laura was a chatterbox, maybe because she had a loud family with three brothers.

"We saw the birdcage," I added. "When you were moving in."

"It died of pneumonia." She took a small bite of her sandwich. "Its name was Robinson."

"Funny name for a bird." Jess picked at her crusts. "And it died?" Jess was the one who organized the funerals when we were little and wrote out the service. We buried them behind the shed in her back yard: two dead hamsters, a field mouse, several dried out lizards, and the remains of her baby blanket. Her father grew the best vegetables on the street.

Sally Noonis folded the paper and plastic bag together in a neat little square and put them back in the brown paper bag. She dusted crumbs off the table and put the paper bag into her backpack.

"What sort of bird was it?" Jess asked.

I thought Jess might upset her with the question but Sally shook her head. "It was a lovebird, blue with yellow on its wings." She put her hands together as though she was still holding it and I felt a lump in my throat. I knew how sad I would feel to lose someone I loved.

Several weeks went by. Sally joined us each day for lunch in the noisy cafeteria. She spoke only when asked a question. "Yes" she was settling in. She liked her house. Her bedroom looked out on the back lawn. Her parents were away a lot, but when we asked where, she shrugged. I thought it would be nice if she asked about us. My Gram was in hospital and my parents gave each other sad looks when I asked about her. Each day Sally brought the same lunch: an egg sandwich and a plastic cup of yogurt in a brown paper bag.

One Friday Sally handed out pink envelopes to each of us. "On Sunday it's my birthday," she said. "You're the only friends I know to ask." I wondered what being friends meant to Sally. Jess and Laura and I had been friends since second grade and we shared everything. We'd only known Sally a few weeks and she really didn't know us at all.

I ripped open my invitation. It wasn't printed up with dates and times like a proper invitation with balloons and paper hats dancing around the edges. The invitation was written in Sally's own handwriting on bright pink notepaper. The envelope was perfumed.

We looked at each other. "I'm not doing anything," I said.

Jess looked at Laura. "Sure we can come," they said. None of us did much on weekends. We hung out together at the park, maybe went to a movie or shared a pizza at Jess's house.

"My parents are away," Sally said. "I'm going to make a cake."

That Saturday, I went with Laura and Jess to the mall. A pet shop there sold every small creature imaginable: puppies and kittens, turtles and fish, and of course, birds. Jess held a gray kitten against her cheek while Laura petted the spaniel puppies in the front playpen. I found my way to the back room where the birds were kept.

"What sort of bird are we looking for?" Jess had followed me and nudged my arm.

"I don't know," I said. We'd always had hamsters and the plastic piping and cage still cluttered the back shed next to my sister's blackened doll house. Once I tried to light a fire in its little iron stove. "You should have known better," Gram had said. I loved Gram but she could be a trial and now she was sick and I didn't like visiting her.

"What are you thinking?" Jess asked.

"She seemed really sad," I said. "Maybe another bird like Robinson would cheer her up."

My parents had explained how losing a pet was one way for kids to learn about death. I wasn't convinced. My grandfather died when he was really old and my grandmother was going to die now because she was really old. And seeing my dead hamsters hadn't taught me anything.

"Cockatiels can learn to talk," Jess trailed her fingers over the cages and the birds hopped from perch to perch. "They're more interesting than lovebirds."

"We should get two." I studied the lovebirds. Some had green feathers, others blue, and their wings were beautifully laced with fine black bars. "Maybe Robinson died from loneliness." I remembered the English woman with the stones in her pockets. Maybe if she'd had some birds to care for, she'd have been okay.

We pooled our money and ended up with two lovebirds and a borrowed cage. Mr. Hall wagged his finger at us as we were leaving. "You girls remember to bring the cage back next weekend." We promised. He knew us.

I swung the cage gently and watched the birds hold their balance on the central swing. "She'll love them," I said. My friends agreed.

On Sunday Laura and Jess came to my house and checked the birds. I'd fed them and they looked happy. "Empty the water dish," my mother suggested. "You don't want a mess and water everywhere." She shooed us out the door. "Just get back in time for supper." She hugged me and her apron smelled of cookie dough. "You sure you're doing the right thing, Frannie?" she asked.

"Its name was Robinson," I said.

"Funny name for a bird," my mother said as she closed the door.

Number eighty-seven looked quiet, blinds drawn, Sunday quiet. "You don't think she's forgotten we were coming." I was feeling a little jittery. The two little birds stared up at me with beady eyes.

We rang the bell.

Sally was dressed in a long white gown like a wedding dress. The skirt was too long so she'd folded the fabric over her belt. She wore white sequined shoes that seemed too large for her feet and a white velvet ribbon held her hair back from her forehead. Strange, I thought, for a Sunday birthday party. We were all thirteen, for heaven's sake. We didn't play dress-up anymore.

"My parents are away." She ushered us into the hallway and through into the dining room. "It's nice to have friends visiting," she said politely. We followed single file. She didn't mention the cage I was holding.

The table was set with four places, flatware and plates, and paper napkins covered with brilliant birds of paradise too beautiful to be used. We each took a chair and shot furtive glances at each other. Laura giggled.

The blinds were drawn and the ceiling lamp was dim. Two thick white candles sat on the table, unlit. I wondered if Sally would light them; some candles smelled good. The house smelled musty like it needed a good spritz of air freshener, and where was Sally's mother?

"Is today really your birthday, Sally?" I asked, because when we had birthdays our mothers made a fuss and put out paper hats and special gifts for everyone, and the room would be light and bright and festive.

"My parents are away," Sally repeated. "I had to prepare everything myself." She stood behind her chair, fair hair hanging straight against her cheeks. "I have a cake in the kitchen," she added. "I'll get it now. It's chocolate with pink icing."

We sat at the table and listened to the silence of the house. Laura picked up the spoon beside her empty bowl. "Ooh, the soup is delicious." She made silly sipping noises. Jess, not to be outdone, tapped her fork against her empty water glass. "Waiter, waiter, bring the food." We were nervous, three teenage girls at a birthday celebration, and no adults in sight.

"Is she coming back?" Laura whispered.

I whispered, too, "I don't think we should be here. It feels weird." The two birds fluttered in the cage at my feet.

"Oh, look!" Jess pointed to the corner of the room where the tall dark sideboard stood. The birdcage hung on its elegant, white metal stand. It had a pot of plastic greenery in the center and trails of ivy hanging down through the wire slats. Jess had been right; it was not made for birds. It looked dusty and gray and lifeless.

Sally returned to the dining room. She carried a cake with bright pink icing and a thin pink candle on a silver tray. She walked slowly, shielding the flame with her hand. The candle sent shadows over her pale face.

"Don't go yet, please." She put the cake down beside her plate. "I have to make a wish."

Sally's story of Robinson was like my little wooden box with the hidden compartment. Empty. She'd never had a bird called Robinson. We had believed her story and spent all our money for nothing.

I picked up the cage and put it on the table. "We brought a birthday present for you."

Sally looked puzzled. "What's that?" she asked.

"You told us your bird died," I said.

Jess stood up so abruptly her chair tipped over. "It wasn't true, was it, Sally?" Her voice sounded wobbly and she didn't try to pick up the chair. She put her spoon down on the table. "It really isn't your birthday, is it?"

"My parents are away." Sally's voice was shrill. The velvet ribbon had slipped back on her head so her hair escaped over one ear. She was out of focus, squinting in the weak light. "It was a lie," she said, "Only a little lie." She tweaked the hair ribbon into place. "Please stay, I have to make a wish before the candle goes out."

We stood silently as Sally closed her eyes and I wondered what she was wishing for. She blew out the candle and a tiny spiral of gray smoke drifted up. She picked up the cake knife with the engraved handle and carefully cut the cake. She placed a slice of cake on each of our plates. "I made the cake specially for today." And she handed the plates down the table.

What could we do? We shuffled our feet and took the cake. Jess picked up her chair and we sat in uncomfortable silence, and no one was willing to break it. The cake was dry and our water glasses were empty. We ate quickly, our forks clinking against the china plates, while Sally sat silently at the head of the table. As soon as I'd swallowed the last bite I picked up the cage with its crushed red bow. "We have to go," I said.

When we arrived at my house, my mother was there at the door. "I was coming to get you," she said. "This whole birthday thing seemed so odd I called a neighbor. Sally's mother is very sick in Gifford Hospital. Her father is trying to manage."

Our kitchen was warm and welcoming and smelled of chocolate chip cookies.

"Why didn't she tell us?" Then I thought of Gram and how I hadn't told my friends how sick she was and why it frightened me to see her knobby old hands holding the top of the hospital blanket.

"What about the birds?" Jess asked.

"I've got some cookies for you," my mother said. "You can return the birds tomorrow."

I thought of the musty room and the pulled blinds, of Sally in her mother's dress making her wish in front of friends. I put my arms around my mother and drew in the smell of fresh-baked cookies. The little lovebirds chirped in the cage at my feet. We'll keep the birds, I thought, just in case Sally gets really lonely and needs them later.

Acknowledgments

I was born in Australia, came to the U.S. in 1972, and with my husband and two children, settled in Hanover, New Hampshire. In 1987, I received an MFA from Vermont College. In 2016, my first book of short stories, *Butcher Bird*, was published.

This book would not be possible without the love and support of many people. I'd like to thank my immediate family for being my first readers, my brother Huon for his enthusiastic support, and my brother Justin who remembers.

Also, I'd like to extend a very special thank you to my friend Joni Cole for her encouragement and sharp eye, and to her circle of writers. Another warm thank you goes to Deborah Heimann, Jessica Moreland of Brigid Book Works, and Jeffrey Zygmont of Free People Publishing for their professional input and support. And my heartfelt thanks to my friends and fellow writers who believed in my stories.